DEADLY CURRENT

Mischievous Malamute Mystery Series Book 4

HARLEY CHRISTENSEN

ISBN: 978-1-952252-06-8

CHAPTER ONE

I'd never seen metal twisted to the point it resembled nothing more than a blackened mass.

And yet, something in the back of my mind prickled as they hoisted it from the unforgiving depths of the ravine. It was the realization it had once possessed a discernible form—one that had propelled its rider into the abyss while it survived the plummet—if survive can be used to describe an inanimate object.

It didn't really matter one way or the other, as the frantic rescue turned into a mission of recovery. It simply existed so that I was forced to bear witness—daring me to look away, all the while knowing I couldn't...

Wouldn't.

Finally, as the screeching of the winch came to a halt, I lowered my gaze, absently shuffling my foot in the dirt before turning and walking away, releasing the power it held over me while resigning me to sift through the aftermath left by its void.

Then again, death has always had a funny way of affecting me like that.

* * *

Seven and a half hours earlier…

"Are you sure you know how to drive a stick?" I asked, gripping the armrest as my best friend, Leah, ground the gears of the convertible that I had, against my better judgment, allowed her to rent in my name.

"Of course I do," she replied, sounding mildly offended. "I'm a natural."

I winced, suddenly worried I was risking my life, along with my hard-earned safe driver benefits so that she could test her mad skills on this obnoxiously gorgeous piece of automotive workmanship. Nicoh howled from the backseat, turning his ninety-eight-pound frame around so that he graced us with his backside. It was just one more way he routinely elected to share his opinion.

"You may want to shut that furball up or I'm dumping him into the ocean the minute we come within sight of a beach." I gave Leah a sideways glance, noting she sounded a tad too gleeful at the prospect, which she confirmed by adding, "And we all know how much he *loves* getting those dainty little tootsies wet." She tilted her head back and released a maniacal laugh.

I flashed to the last time we'd attempted to give him a bath, momentarily reflecting on the fact it hadn't gone terribly well—for humans or canine—just as she managed to jam the shifter into the proper gear.

Suddenly, we were skidding around the corner, weaving precariously close to the sidewalk, where several pedestrians dove for cover. I stopped holding my breath and released my grip on the armrest ever so slightly as she merged into the freeway traffic, nodding at the Staples Center in the distance as we passed.

"Mmm…mmm… Gotta love those hockey players."

As long as she kept her hands securely on the wheel I didn't care, though after a moment of reflecting on that comment, felt it warranted a response. "You don't even follow hockey."

"Yeah, but you've gotta admit, they look pretty cute in those outfits." This time, her tone was insistent, which made me face her.

"Honestly, Leah, guys tend to prefer the term 'uniform' over 'outfits.'" She grunted her concession, as I prattled on. "Though in hockey, they refer to the jerseys as sweaters, so as that's an article of clothing you are familiar with, perhaps you aren't a lost cause after all."

She nodded, her brow creased, as though absorbing the knowledge I was so generously sharing. I decided to take full advantage. "And, in case you were interested, we do have a team back in Arizona…and the players are a whole lot cuter."

Leah smiled broadly. "Oh yeah, the Cardinals…I've seen some of those boys in action."

I think I almost crushed my molar formulating a response. "That's the football team."

"Ooooh…football players," she replied. "They're cute in their little sweaters, too."

"Coyotes," I growled under my breath, ignoring the fashion faux pas, as this was one of the rare occasions the topic was clearly lost on her.

"What?" Leah asked, nearly crashing the convertible in the process as she craned her neck from side to side, in search of the four-legged variety.

I gripped the dashboard. "Arizona Coyotes—the name of our hockey team."

"I know." She winked before shoving the shifter into the next gear, squealing with delight as we surged forward and Nicoh resumed his howling.

I could only shake my head as I looked back and forth at the two of them.

The things I put up with for friends.

Still, I appreciated her attempted distraction. This entire trip— which had been her idea—had ultimately been one, masqueraded behind the guise of a part sight-seeing, part wedding location scout for our friend, Anna Goodwin.

Leah had none-to-gently informed me that my whine card had expired and I had developed a permanent frowny face that made both small children and puppies whimper and run for cover. In a nutshell, I was no longer allowed to remain in the persistent state of funk, moping around as though my reason to live had ceased to exist.

I'll admit, there was a bit of residue left behind from the unceremonious departure of a not-to-be-named homicide detective, as well as from a biological father named Martin, who had gone from Jack-in-the-Box to phantom almost overnight. Granted, the latter was an upgrade, as he had been MIA for the better part of my life, but both men had left me moody, snarky and downright obstinate, forcing Leah to take matters into her own hands.

We finally arrived at the imposing glass and metal structure where Anna worked as a private investigator at Stanton Investigations, alongside two of our other friends, Abe and Elijah Stanton. Anna had been their office manager extraordinaire from the beginning when the two brothers joined forces. As they took on more clients, she earned her own P.I. license. And while she was more than capable of doing both her office duties in addition to tackling her own cases, Abe and Elijah insisted she hire an assistant so they could bring her into an investigative role full-time.

Neither of us had been to the new office since they'd moved, though a pang of nostalgia hit me when I thought of the tiny space they occupied in the back of an insurance agency. The building had recently been torn down to accommodate a business complex but the Stantons had already been looking for a new place to hang their shingle as their business had outgrown the small office.

Leah maneuvered the convertible up to the entrance of the

parking structure, where a mechanical-sounding voice recited the location of an unoccupied spot before opening the gate and granting us permission to proceed.

"Swanky," she murmured.

"Indeed," I replied, while Nicoh snorted his approval from the backseat. "Up and at 'em boy." I swatted him on the butt and received an annoyed grunt for my efforts.

After tucking ourselves into the designated parking space, we rode the elevator in silence and exited at the main floor, where we were greeted by a portly uniformed guard, positioned securely behind an expansive marble fortress of a desk. His name badge said "Louis."

"Hi, we're here to see—" I started.

"Hold on, you can't come here with *that*." The guard frowned, pointing at Nicoh.

I ignored him and pressed on. "We're here to see Anna Goodwin from Stanton Investigations. That's on the seventeenth floor, correct?"

His eyes widened in surprise. "Abe and Elijah's girl? The one that looks like a supermodel?"

I nodded, elbowing Leah when she rolled her eyes at the mention of "girl."

The guard rubbed his chin. "Hey, isn't Blaze Edwards her fiancé?"

"You know Blaze?" I worked to keep the surprise out of my voice. Epic fail.

"Oh, *come on*." He released an obnoxious snort. "He's like only the most famous extreme sports dude since like…well, ev-ah…" He completed that thought with a thumb and pinky "hang loose" gesture combined with a swivel of his hips, which was met with an audible gag from Leah.

While that moniker had been true for the better part of his teens and twenties, a career-ending injury had forced Blaze to hang up his surfboard for a gig producing and directing environmental documentaries.

I decided it was best not close the opening he'd offered and instead, used it to my benefit. "Then surely you should recognize one of the stars of his most-watched YouTube videos?" When the guard frowned as he glanced between the two of us, I sighed and tilted my head at Nicoh. "Not us. Him. You know, Bucko?"

"The surfing dog?" I nodded as he surveyed Nicoh, who sat at attention, eying the bowl of candy that sat just within nose reach on the marble desk. "I loved that video, but wasn't it about a German Shepherd, named Rocco? This dog looks like something —else."

Leah waved a hand at him. "Obviously, you don't know your breeds very well, Louis. And for the record, she did say Rocco." He gave her a doubtful look, so she offered him a three-finger salute. "Was right here, Louis. Scout's honor."

Louis shook his head. "I don't know. I don't remember the dog in the video being so fat—"

"Shh—he's a little sensitive about his recent weight gain," I interjected, placing a finger across my lips and casting a sympathetic glance in Nicoh's direction. "Girlfriend issues. We prefer the term 'fluffy,'" I whispered as Leah nodded her agreement, though her lips trembled as she fought to keep from laughing.

"Still, I don't know," he replied, putting his hands on his hips.

We were quickly losing this battle to Louis the portly authority.

Leah stepped in. "Well, as Mr. Edwards' assistant, I'd hate to have to report that you wouldn't allow us to deliver a very special gift to his girlfriend."

"What's the dog got to do with it?" Louis frowned.

"Singing telegram from her favorite tv star." Leah graced him with an award-winning deadpan.

"The dog sings?" Louis peered skeptically at Nicoh, who, to

his benefit, was now on his best behavior, quietly sitting on his haunches, his ginormous head held high.

"What did you think—that Rocco was a one-trick pooch?" Leah replied, waving a hand dismissively. "Everyone in the business has to have more than one skill up their keister nowadays."

Before Louis could request an impromptu performance, I added, "Yeah, we're on a tight schedule, have a lot of happiness to spread today, so we'll get out your hair and be on our way." I grabbed Nicoh's lead and headed toward the elevators.

"Sorry, Miss, those are down for maintenance for a few more hours," Louis yelled after us. "You'll have to take the stairs."

I stifled a groan. Of course we would. I sighed, not looking forward to having to coax Nicoh up seventeen flights.

A petite blonde in a button-down shirt and jeans rose from her desk when we finally entered the office of Stanton Investigations. I hadn't met Anna's assistant in person but had spoken to her on several occasions and found her to be as personable as she was efficient.

"You must be AJ and Leah." She came around, gripped each of our hands and gave us warm smiles before kneeling to let Nicoh sniff her hand. When he nudged her repeatedly, she giggled and scruffed his head. "And of course, this is *the* Nicoh. Hey, buddy, I'm Sarah. It's so nice to finally meet you all."

"You too, Sarah. It's nice to put a face to the friendly voice on the other end of the connection," I replied. "I should probably warn you, Anna's been shouting your praises from the rooftops."

"Likewise," she replied, chuckling. "By the way, she's really been looking forward to your visit. Come on, I'll give you the official tour." She led us around the spacious new digs, which were tastefully decorated with the touches only Anna's careful eye could have provided. She knocked as we entered a massive open office where Sarah had noted that Abe, Elijah and Anna did their brainstorming. "Hey, Boss. Guess who's here?"

I sucked in a breath of horror as the friend who I professed to know so well had morphed, not only physically but emotionally, into a creature I barely recognized.

It was obvious that she had lost weight. The once jaw-dropping curves had been reduced to skin and bone, given the way her clothes resembled hand-me-downs from an older sibling. Based on their wrinkled, haggard condition—it was also hard to ignore that they appeared to have been repeatedly slept in.

Her long raven locks were knotted in a messy bun that flopped off to the side under the weight, with strands jutting out from every direction, giving it a bristly porcupine appearance.

Bags under her eyes suggested she hadn't slept for some time and while their redness could have been from long hours spent poring over case files or staring at a computer screen, I suspected otherwise.

She was void of makeup and the paleness of her skin combined with hollows beneath her cheekbones made her overall appearance even more pronounced.

Her current state also extended to her usually immaculate, organized surroundings, which looked as though a windstorm had blown through—papers, books and file boxes covered every surface and the remnants of several days' worth of food had long been forgotten. One of the cushions on the loveseat was scrunched against the armrest, suggesting someone had been using it for a makeshift bed.

I shouldn't have been the least bit surprised when Leah blurted out, "What in the hell happened to you?"

Apparently, when they made Leah, tact failed to make its way into the recipe.

I withheld commentary but offered Anna a sympathetic glance to atone for my best friend's big mouth.

Like I said, what I did for friends.

CHAPTER TWO

Fortunately, Anna was not the least bit offended. And though she laughed as she pulled us both into an embrace, it did little to alleviate my shock when pointy shoulder blades nudged my hands. I winced, noting how small she actually seemed compared to her nearly six-foot frame.

"So, how're things…going?" Leah asked, her face twisting into a grimace as she worked to formulate the appropriate question on her second attempt.

Knowing her as well as I did, it took a lot of stretching.

Anna released a small chuckle that sounded a bit sad, glancing down at the pile that covered her desk. "Good…good. Business is good. The boys are busy….on a big job in Vegas. All's good. Everyone's happy."

"Not everyone," Leah replied, causing a tiny shudder to erupt from Anna's shoulders as she continued looking down, her head almost touching her chest.

"Anna, we're asking as your friends," I added. "We want to know…how're things…with *you*?"

Anna lifted her chin ever so slightly before pulling the bun loose, allowing her hair to cascade down her shoulders. After a long moment, she closed the office door, collapsed into a chair and stared out the window.

Leah and I each took a seat opposite her, while Nicoh settled on the floor.

"It's Blaze," she replied after a few moments of awkward silence.

"What—is he okay?" Leah and I asked, our voices echoing through the office.

In Blaze's previous profession, the risks were high and the danger extreme, often proving deadly for a few of his comrades.

She waved us off. "Physically, he's fine…but emotionally… mentally? He seems to have gotten a proverbial case of cold feet." After taking in our raised brows, she added, "I think he's cheating on me."

I shook my head. "No way—Blaze adores you."

I had witnessed this adoration first hand—beaming when she entered the room, enraptured by her every word—pulling her close as though having her near made him complete. It was clear to everyone within a three-mile radius that the couple was far more than in love—they were in love with life, together.

Anna shrugged, still staring out the window.

"I suppose he does…did. Anyway, now that I've finally managed to get you all the way here, let's not allow my overactive imagination to spoil your visit." She pursed her lips and shook her head, before adding, "Just forget I brought it up."

"Nuh, uh, Anna. Be straight with us. If something's bad enough to have reduced you to"—Leah waved her hand around the room, then at Anna—"then we're not going to 'just forget' it. I mean seriously, *you're* the P.I. here. Why don't you just share your evidence with us so we can pick holes in your theory?"

Anna released a weak chuckle. "Okay, you caught me. By the way, that was quite a wicked trick, using my newly-minted P.I. credentials against me."

"I try my best," Leah replied, looking a bit self-satisfied. "Now, please tell us…what's got you so worked up and—not to come off sounding insensitive or judgey—looking downright wretched?"

Fortunately, Anna didn't seem to care, as she took the comment in stride.

"It sounds cliché but when you put things into perspective…" She blew out a long breath, shaking her head as she glanced at the ceiling. "First, it was the late night meetings. Soon, he became more and more distracted, was missing our date nights and when he did manage to show up, he was uncharacteristically late and agitated, as though it was an inconvenience and he had more important places to be.

"As you both know, he's not an angry or mean-spirited person—actually quite the opposed, always so calm and laid back but lately, I can't say or do anything without eliciting a rude, even vicious, remark. No matter how I try to rectify whatever it is that I've done to aggravate him, he snaps at me for no reason."

"Could this new project be causing him more stress?" I asked. "You did mention that the transition was a bit rough, that not everyone he previously worked with was thrilled about the shift and that several of them walked away when he made the announcement."

Anna shook her head. "Blaze realized he was getting older and wasn't going to be able to do that stuff forever, despite what his crew or fans wanted. And if we wanted a family, which I thought he did, he wasn't willing to continue taking those kinds of risks."

She rose, moved to the window and wrapped her arms around her middle. "Oh sure, you see those families where the whole lot is into it and they haul the kids all over the world trying to grasp onto every last bit of adrenaline that comes with it, but for Blaze the thrill had slowly been wearing thin over the years, especially after he lost a couple of his best friends.

"So when this new opportunity arose—one that allowed him to use his current skill set in new ways…ways that could make a real difference to future generations…" Her thought trailed off and she was silent for a long moment before finishing, "No, if the project was stressing him out, his reaction would have been much different…a short period of vocal frustration, followed by a shift to dogged persistence until he was able to mitigate, if not eliminate the issue.

"Instead, he's been stand-offish, even when I try to give him a hug or a simple peck on the cheek. We have separate condos but until recently, he'd pretty much stayed over every night. In fact, we talked about him giving his up until we could find a home after the wedding. That being said, I don't think he's even stepped foot across the threshold of mine in four months and when we do meet, it's always somewhere different and tucked out of the way—places we typically don't even go—and shortly after arriving, he's already eager to be on his way."

"Blaze's behavior may not be related to issues with the project but it also does not lead directly to infidelity," Leah replied. "Why even make the leap to cheating?"

I nodded. "When we last spoke, you mentioned Blaze was having problems getting some of the necessary permits. Couldn't that have something to do with the way he's been acting? You also said he didn't want to have to reach out to his family for help pushing things through. Perhaps he's feeling pressure—from somewhere—to do so?" I paused, before adding, "I agree with Leah. I just don't see Blaze as the cheating type—definitely not on you."

"I wouldn't have thought so either until I saw it with my own eyes," she replied, frowning.

I glanced at Leah. "Saw what with you own eyes?"

"The other woman."

Anna reached into a leather tote bag sitting on the floor and pulled out a file folder. From it, she extracted the contents and tossed them on the desk. A few shifted off the edge and I caught them before they fell and got an eye-full of what had put our friend on high alert.

Leah and I pulled our chairs forward and after I placed the stray photos alongside the others, we peered at each shot.

Blaze and a voluptuous blonde in a fitted black pantsuit, dining in what appeared to be an outside bistro on sunny California day.

Blaze and the same woman, sharing drinks at the bar inside a crowded dance club.

Blaze and the woman, in a random parking lot.

Blaze and the woman, this time clad in leather riding gear, outside a biker bar, their heads bent together.

For each scenario, there were dozens of shots. There were no date or time stamps but clearly, there had been several meetings between the two. Nothing, however, about any of them that suggested intimacy or even a budding relationship.

"One of his employees?" Leah suggested after we gave each image a second glance.

"Not to my knowledge. In fact, I've met most of them over the years and none of them have ever looked like *this*," Anna replied, her tone sour as she stabbed at one of the images. "And did I mention that this is only a sampling of their activities?"

"Who took these?" Leah asked.

Anna looked away, but not before her pale complexion was mottled with red splotches.

Leah nodded and for once, thought before speaking. "Okay, so you've spent a lot of time tailing the two of them—what about when they're not together? Did you follow her or get any details that could help identify her or that explain why Blaze is spending so much time with her?"

Anna shook her head. "She's good...never leaving any tracks...always disappearing into the shadows. Either that or maybe Abe and Elijah have overestimated my abilities. I'm probably going to need to take a leave of absence, anyway, to deal with this. Perhaps I should consider making it permanent." She sighed, before adding, "I was just hoping I'd get it all handled before they returned and before I had to divulge all of my dirty laundry."

"Did you confront Blaze about her or show him...these?" I gestured toward the pictures.

"Gawd, no." Anna pressed her eyes shut and frowned.

"What about Abe and Elijah? Did you share any of your suspicions with them?" I asked, wondering how her change in appearance had escaped their notice, but decided this was not the time to bring it up.

"Double Gawd, no. You've seen Blaze. They'd snap him in half."

Both Leah and I nodded. That was probably true. While Blaze was no twig and was an exceptional athlete, he was no match for a pair of former collegiate-level football players. And, knowing how the Stantons doted over Anna—treating her as they would a sister—they would have crushed him first and asked questions later.

"I don't know, Anna. I still think you should talk to Blaze."

Anna pursed her lips at my suggestion and started to answer when there was a knock at the door. Sarah popped her head in.

"I'm sorry to interrupt but there's someone here to see you. She said it was important."

Anna frowned. "I don't have any appointments scheduled this afternoon."

"No, she confirmed she didn't have one but said it was imperative that she see you," the assistant replied.

"Did she at least provide you with a name?" Anna asked.

Sarah shook her head. "She wouldn't say."

Anna blew out a breath and pulled her hair into a ponytail. "Fine. Give me five minutes and then bring her back."

"Sure thing, Boss." Sarah started to exit but looked back and added, "I should probably note, she's kind of…scary."

"Scary?" Anna blinked. "As in we need to call the police scary?"

"Noooo, more like I'd-rather-kick-your-butt-in-a-cage-fight-than-allow-you-to-waste-any-more-air-or-space scary."

"Uh, thanks for the clarification, I think?" Anna let out a small chuckle as Sarah closed the door behind her.

"What do you make of that?" Leah asked.

"Who knows—you see all types in this business," Anna replied, straightening her clothes and pulling on a blazer before attempting to make her office a bit more presentable.

We had just helped her tuck the last of the mess away when there was a knock at the door and Sarah re-entered with the visitor in tow—a tall, formidably built, sun-bronzed goddess in her late twenties to early thirties.

A mane of platinum cornrows cascaded down her back and ended at her waist, where they were loosely tied with several black leather strands. The combination of her hair and deep tan made her eyes her most striking—and unnerving—feature, a blue so light it could have easily been carved from ice. She was clad head-to-toe in leather riding gear, which seemed unseasonably warm but given the way she perused each of us, I wondered if anything warm ran through her veins.

After Sarah exited, the visitor strode across the room, stuck out her hand and started to speak, when Anna surprised us by ignoring her outstretched hand, instead opting to slap her hard across the face.

When that yielded no response, Anna surprised us again.

This time, she slugged the woman, hitting her squarely, in the jaw.

CHAPTER THREE

I heard Leah suck in a breath just as I did, awaiting the fallout, but after cracking her jaw, the visitor simply smirked as she reached into the inside pocket of her motorcycle jacket, extracted a thin wallet and attempted to hand it to Anna, who crossed her arms defiantly and stared the woman down.

"Uh, Anna, is everything okay?" Leah asked as we glanced back and forth between them.

Even Nicoh had risen and was now positioning himself protectively between the two, ready for action.

"No, Leah, everything is most definitely not okay," Anna replied through gritted teeth. It was as fierce as I'd ever seen her. "It's *her*."

It was like being late to the party. I glanced at Leah, who shrugged at me, before responding, "You've lost us. Her who?"

Anna broke the gaze, rounded her desk and pulled one of the files we'd just stashed from its hiding place. "The witch in the pictures," she seethed, before thrusting the photos, one by one, on the desk so that we had a full view of each.

The visitor looked down, only mildly interested. She continued to offer the wallet and Anna still refused to accept.

Leah and I peered at each image of Blaze and the woman Anna believed he'd been trading more than digits with.

"She's wearing a wig in the photos," Anna clarified, "and accentuated some of her more…feminine assets."

This time, Leah and I glanced from the pictures to the woman, each of us gasping at the transformation. The woman standing in front of us looked more like Ronda Rousey's supersized twin than the voluptuous, heavily made-up blonde with satiny locks that Blaze had met on at least a dozen occasions.

The bemused smirk on the real-life version was starting to annoy me. "She doesn't seem all that surprised to learn you were following her, Anna."

The woman shrugged and started to respond when Anna thrust a finger at her. "You…do not get to speak. You're on my turf and I'll let you know when I'm ready to hear your sorry-ass excuse for showing your face."

Anna moved from behind the desk and positioned herself millimeters from the woman's side and for a split-second, I thought round two was about to begin when the visitor, still holding the wallet, calmly responded, "Blaze is in trouble."

Anna leaned in and snarled into the woman's ear, "You'd better believe those fake boobs he's in trouble."

The gal smirked and again thrust the wallet at her. "My private investigator's license. Name's Decker. Kelly Decker. Blaze hired me to look into the recent…incidents."

As Anna's eyes widened and she took a step back, the bad juju that had been swirling throughout the office seemed to evaporate.

"You're Decker?" She backed up another step and gave the woman a thorough once-over before nodding. "I've heard of you…from Abe and Elijah. But you don't look crusty, have a smoker's voice…or appear to be male."

Decker barely moved a muscle but somewhere a snort

resounded. "That was my pops. Recently passed away from smoking those arsenic logs he called cigars. I started working with him when I was ten and took over the business when the cancer finally took him down." There was a hitch in her voice when she added," Man was a bulldog…all the way until the savage end."

"I'm very sorry to hear about your father," Anna replied quietly, as Leah and I nodded.

"It is what it is. Life goes on." Decker shrugged. "Mind if I take off my jacket, sit down and have a normal adult conversation?"

Anna nodded and gestured toward the sofa as Decker peeled off her jacket, exposing a pair of guns so chiseled I muttered a word of thanks that I hadn't been the one who'd slugged her—though it did give Anna a few extra gummy bears in my book. I broke free of my internal dialogue when I caught a glimpse of a tattoo on the inside of Decker's wrist as she tossed the jacket over her knee.

Aequitas.

Justice.

Interesting.

Decker got right down to business. "I assume that we can speak freely in front of Arianna and Leah?"

Leah and I might have been shocked this stranger knew our identities but I had to give Anna cred—she played it as cool as a glacier, offering Decker nothing more than a single head nod.

Decker grunted before continuing, "Great. For several months now, Blaze has been the target of a series of incidents at home and work. His crew, too. At first, they seemed to be isolated coincidences, but when they started occurring more frequently and evolved from pranks to increasingly menacing episodes, a few of the crew bailed when the threats extended to their families."

"Threats? Blaze didn't mention any of this to me," Anna replied, looking down as she chewed her lip.

"He didn't want to worry you. He knew the moment he said something, you'd make it your sole mission. Plus, he worried about what those Stanton boys would do if they found out."

"You know Abe and Elijah?" Anna raised her head.

Decker shrugged. "Everyone knows those two. Blaze got my number from them—he asked for the best—and he got me."

It was a statement of fact, not arrogance.

I didn't know her credentials but if the Stantons thought she was that good, there was no question, despite whatever ego she was bringing to the table.

At the same time, I found myself shaking my head. If Anna had only shown the photos to Abe and Elijah, she would have known what she was up against. I wondered why they wouldn't have mentioned Blaze's request. I also started wondering whether Decker was a mind-reader when she responded to my internal ramblings.

"When Blaze contacted Abe and Elijah, he only indicated he needed help with his current project, so as far as they knew, the services he required could have simply involved looking into perspective employees' or vendors' backgrounds. Or at the financial standing of potential backers. At no time did he mention the incidents that had been occurring.

"Having said that, once things began to escalate, I encouraged him to have a conversation with you and the Stantons, but he was adamant that none of you were to be brought into the fold, at least not until he could get a handle on these threats. As it is, he could fire me for getting you involved now."

"So why are you here, then?" Anna asked, frowning.

"My rationale is two-fold. While I have always believed Blaze should have told you about these occurrences from the very beginning, I now feel *not* telling you could prove catastrophic. If you don't know a threat exists, how are you able to protect yourself when it's sitting on your doorstep?"

"I completely agree," Anna replied. "You said your reasons were two-fold?"

Decker nodded. "I don't often ask but when I do, I get the best. And from what I've heard from the Stantons—their own qualifications notwithstanding—you're it."

"You're asking for *my* assistance?" Anna's tone turned incredulous as she furrowed her brow.

"I am. This…thing is quickly getting out of hand. Sooner or later someone is going to get seriously hurt, or worse." Decker paused, crossing her arms. "Yet Blaze refuses to get the police involved and the crew that remains agree, even though they don't know where the threat is coming from, they want to handle it internally."

"Surely they realize they can't deal with it themselves? And, if things continue to escalate, the police are going to involve themselves, regardless of what Blaze or his crew wants," Leah replied.

Decker shrugged. "A lot of them have not had positive experiences where law enforcement is concerned."

I nodded. Anna had previously told us that Blaze and his friends had a few run-ins as juveniles.

"What about Blaze's family—I assume he hasn't told them either?" Anna asked, blowing out a breath when Decker shook her head. "As usual, I'm sure he was concerned about his father's propensity to get over-involved or turn it into some media sideshow." This time Decker was silent. "Unless Blaze believes his father is directly involved in the threats, that is?"

It had been no secret that Terrence Edwards had been less than pleased by his son's choice of career paths, including his most current venture.

"Blaze doesn't believe any member of his family has had any

involvement," Decker replied, standing as she eased into her moto jacket before adding, "Though I prefer to keep my options for potential suspects open, as my expectations of my fellow beings, especially ones with ulterior motives, tend to be fairly low."

Anna nodded. "You mentioned needing help."

Decker grunted. "First, I need to let Blaze know that I've breached our agreement, allow him to either digest it or fire me."

"Let me handle that," Anna suggested.

Decker frowned, shaking her head. "I prefer to do my own dirty work."

"Indulge me, would you?" Anna tone was insistent. "He's my fiancé. I know him best."

"Fine," Decker replied. "Just let me know when it's done."

Anna gave her a single head nod and Decker relayed her cell phone number and extended a hand to each of us. I was initially worried she'd crush my hand with those meat hooks but found her embrace to be firm and no-nonsense, much like the woman delivering it.

There was a moment of silence as we watched Decker exit. Leah was the first to fill the void.

"What's the plan, Boss—get the story direct from the horse's mouth?"

"Sure," Anna grumbled, grabbing her tote and striding toward the door. "Right after I find him and kick him in the ass."

CHAPTER FOUR

"Um, are you sure you want us as your wing chicks?" Leah asked as Anna revved the engine of her monster SUV and punched the gas, surging us forward as we exited the parking garage and merged into L.A. traffic.

"Honestly, I'd feel better if you came with me," Anna replied, sounding less and less like the bright and cheerful girl we had come to know and love.

Then again, even the most well-grounded, even-keeled person had their tipping points. I certainly didn't fault her for being human and was actually glad we were present when Decker had dealt the blow.

"What's the deal with Decker, anyway?" I hoped my question wasn't going to send our friend over the edge.

Thankfully, Anna released her stranglehold on the steering wheel.

"According to Abe and Elijah, Decker's father was the real deal. An old school gumshoe and a real son-of-a-gun ball buster," she replied, her eyes bright as she relayed their telling of the story. "He started doing skip traces but the detective bug was in his blood. He was a natural—one of those guys who relied on his gut

—always fair but tough. And he never quit until he had his man, solved the case or had whatever answers his client's sought."

"Must run in his daughter's blood, too," Leah replied. "She seems…intense."

"Yeah, she's a different beast, all right. Guess Sarah had it right after all, about her being a bit 'rough' around the edges," Anna replied.

Once again, I was glad I hadn't been the one hurling the accusations at Decker. Given her physical size, stature and general demeanor, she seemed like she could knock a few heads together. Still, she'd brushed Anna's comments off with ease, as though slicking off water in a rainstorm. Tough with thick skin and intensely focused on the task at hand and yet, willing to break ranks when the situation necessitated it, at great risk to her pocketbook and reputation.

I closed the chapter on my mental meanderings as Anna continued, "I remember Abe and Elijah telling me that old man Decker was always hell-bent on some mission—that there were stories of pre- and post-Decker—and in the last thirty years of his life, he was ruthless. He would act first, question and work the specifics out later. He was of the mindset that there were enemies, monsters and evil everywhere and that the concept of good was nothing but a myth."

"Any idea what happened?" Leah asked.

"Yeah, it's actually a famous Los Angeles crime story. I'm sure you heard about it when one of those investigative shows did an anniversary feature on it?" We both shook our heads. "Decker's wife was murdered thirty years ago. Killer was never found. L.A.P.D. had Decker in their sights for a while, but he was cleared due to a lack of evidence. Many believed it was a retribution hit, that Decker had crossed someone—the wrong someone—but he emphatically denied it, swearing that his wife's killer would be brought to justice, even if he had to do it from Hell."

"Whoa," Leah replied.

Anna nodded and continued, "His wife's attack was beyond brutal. Her throat had been cut so deeply her head was barely attached. The killer had also ripped her open like an animal, splaying her insides across the bed and coating every surface with blood. But that's not even the worst of it." Anna sucked in a breath as she merged onto the freeway. "When law enforcement arrived—an anonymous call had tipped them off—they found the couple's daughter clinging to her mother's body."

"Decker?" Both Leah and I asked simultaneously.

"Yes, it took the police quite a while to coax her from the room—to leave her mother—and then to even speak but when she did, she told the officers that she had been hiding under the bed and only come out once she was sure her mother's attacker was gone. Upon seeing her mother, she climbed on the bed and tried to comfort her. Of course, there was nothing that could be done but Decker refused to leave her."

"Kind of explains things," I murmured, thinking about the way Decker had presented herself.

I wondered if she lived in the shadows of her father's legacy —serving as his warrior—existing to see his visions to fruition. Would she spend a lifetime trying to bring her mother's murderer to justice? Having seen Decker in the flesh, I already knew—and understood—her answer, but in the end, would it be worth the cost?

Those of us that had experienced death, violence…even murder had to answer that in our own way and in our own time. But at some point, we had to take weights and measures. Not for ourselves or those whose justice we sought, but for ones who lived and that we loved—those who deserved to live without constant fear or worry for the day when our toll came due.

And at the end of the day I had Leah and Nicoh. And our friends—Anna, Abe, Elijah—even Ramirez.

I hoped Kelly Decker had the same type of support system but, in truth, I had to wonder if she even entertained the notion.

"I guess," Anna responded. "You think that's where she gets her toughness?"

"Probably," I replied, staring out the window at the city that buzzed and went on, in spite of us mere mortals.

Nicoh nudged my hand, as though sensing my mood. I stroked his satiny fur and he grumbled out a low "whoo-woo."

"Where are we headed?" Leah asked.

I noted that her demeanor had down-shifted considerably after the discussion of Decker's mother.

"To the beach." Anna offered us each a sideways look. "You two sure you're up for it?"

Leah slapped her leg and pasted on a smile. "Honey, we're from the desert, we're always up for something beachy."

"Well, here's to sand in your shorts, then," Anna replied, her tone dry.

I wasn't sure about the sentiment but truth be told, it didn't sound all that appealing.

We drove for what seemed like hours along the Pacific Coast Highway and while Leah and I had made the trek on various occasions, we made small talk with Anna, asking her a variety of questions about the area we already knew the answers to—just to fill the void and occupy her mind—with the hope we could temper down her emotions before she confronted Blaze.

Mind you, we were on her side, so it wasn't our place to question why he'd done what he had but I gave him some credit—he'd been smart enough to get a reference from the Stantons—but failing to inform his fiancé? If he had been my brother, I would have kicked him in the teeth. If he'd been my fiancé…well, I can't say what I'd do, not having been in similar circumstances.

I couldn't disagree with Anna's reaction. I'd probably feel the same. Especially after Blaze had hired an investigator under her nose months earlier, not to mention how his entire response to the threats had affected her—mentally, emotionally and physically. I only hoped at the end of this, we would understand the rationale behind his decision—and that all of us hadn't played him wrong from the start.

We pulled into one of the beach communities that was popular with locals but had yet to attract the masses. According to Anna, the few that lived there full time hoped to keep it that way. The ecosystem had suffered in the last several decades and the constant threat of development only served to further its decline.

"Blaze's filming a segment of the documentary here," Anna commented, her tone somber. "Soon, it'll all be gone—a resort community is scheduled to be built, right there." She pointed at an outcropping, where the beach was stopped by a rocky cliff.

"Ah, lovely beach views," Leah replied, pursing her lips as she added, "for the most elite and privileged of the upper echelon."

"Isn't that the way it always goes?" Anna sounded equally bitter.

"That's why Blaze chose it as a topic for his documentary, though...to bring awareness?" I asked, in a feeble attempt to lighten the mood.

Anna pulled off her shoes and buried her feet in the sand. "In large part...yes. He wanted to use his name and his brand in a positive way to generate awareness of the continued annihilation of beaches, wildlife and sea life in support of capitalism."

"Kind of controversial subject matter, wouldn't you say?" Leah added, pulling her own shoes off.

Anna nodded. "It is. Fortunately, Blaze has the backing of the surfing community and the locals."

"But it could also be the reason he and his crew have been targeted," I thought out loud.

"Maybe so." Anna nodded.

"Has anything like this happened in the past?" I asked.

"Just the usual overzealous fans," she replied, before adding, "but nothing that could be construed as menacing."

"I'd like to know the specifics of the threats Decker mentioned," Leah commented.

"So would I." Anna looked at us both before kicking a pile of sand. "So would I."

We trudged about a half of a mile up the beach, where a large tent had been erected in the sand. Angry voices buzzed from inside the covering before a tanned guy wearing cargo shorts and a fluorescent yellow surfing shirt stormed out, running his hands through his shoulder length hair. He muttered something under his breath and nearly ran into us before he'd looked up.

"Oh hey, Anna. I didn't know you were coming out today." His frown suggested he wasn't going to be part of the welcoming committee.

"Hey, Bryce," Anna replied. "Actually, the trip wasn't planned but something has come up that I need to discuss with Blaze." She nodded at the tent. "Everything okay?"

He glanced at us before looking over his shoulder, the downward turn of his mouth increasing two-fold before he responded. "Chalk it up to creative differences."

"You sure?" Anna pressed.

"Yeah, I'm sure. Why're you asking?" Bryce turned his focus to the surfers on the horizon, working his jaw as he chewed the inside of his mouth.

Anna continued to survey him. "No reason. Could just hear you guys all the way up the beach—must be some pretty significant 'creative differences.'"

Bryce shrugged. "Just the usual. You know how much of a perfectionist Blaze is. Wind condition has to be right. Natural lighting has to be just so. It's hard to get Mother Nature to see things your way when she's the one in control."

"You're sure that's all it is?" The harder Anna pushed him, the more shifting he did from one foot the other.

"Second time you asked, Anna. Second time I'm saying yes," Bryce replied, this time his voice was laced with a bit of venom and sarcasm. "You want a better answer than that, then I suggest you talk to your fiancé." He thrust his hands in his pockets, brushing past us as he continued up the beach.

"Nice dude," Leah mumbled.

"Normally he is," Anna replied, looking after him. "Bryce Denton is Blaze's best friend and right-hand man."

"He's certainly not a very convincing liar." My response did nothing to hide my first impression of Blaze's bestie.

"No, he is not." Anna nodded at the tent. "Shall we go to the source?"

"You're still sure you want us to tag along?" I asked.

"Why? Are you worried?" Anna gave me a sideways glance.

"Well, I don't think AJ was asking if you needed witnesses," Leah replied. "So if you didn't want anyone to see what's about to go down in there, perhaps it might be best if we stayed out here."

"Chicken." Anna snorted. "Don't worry. I'm not going to do anything rash." She glanced over her shoulder before entering the tent. "At least not until after he's spilled his guts."

I slid a cautious look at Leah as we followed her into the tent, where several people were standing around a large folding table covered with maps and various aerial photographs. A few of them looked up, shifting just enough that Blaze became visible, oblivious to our arrival as he continued studying the materials.

"…and that's why it's imperative that we wait to shoot this until we can ensure the security of the people involved."

Sun-bleached waves swarmed his head, his lapis eyes bright with excitement as he talked with his hands. Lines crinkled at the corners of his eyes as he squinted and pointed at one section of the map, his tanned fingers scarred from his former occupation.

Suddenly, his eyes flickered in our direction and the moment he caught a glimpse of Anna, it was as though time froze and the only energy or movement of space and time existed between them. He rounded the table and within steps, embraced her in a warm hug, giving her a peck on the forehead as he did.

"Hey, Babe. I didn't know you were coming out today, and with company, to boot." Blaze gave us a quick hug and knelt to scratch Nicoh's ears, a necessary distraction from the tension that swirled—and continued to mount—as Anna narrowed her eyes at him.

"Just saw Bryce on our way in," she replied, ignoring his comment. "Didn't seem himself."

Blaze would not meet her gaze as he shrugged. "He's under a lot of pressure. Just needed some time to cool off."

"Huh, sounds like all of you are under a lot of pressure." Anna crossed her arms and tapped her foot, causing a few of Blaze's crew to slowly back away from the table.

"Nothing more than the usual," Blaze replied, frowning as he added, "though in hindsight, we probably bit off more than we can chew with this project—should have started it three months earlier than we did."

"According to Bryce, sounds like you're having more than a few timing issues." This time Anna's voice was sharp.

"What do you mean?" Bryce asked, his eyes going wide as he absorbed Anna's stance and demeanor. "Crap. You talked to Decker."

No verbal response was needed on Anna's part—her expression was enough to suck all the air out of the tent.

CHAPTER FIVE

Leah and I shuffled our feet, alongside the crew, and exchanged relieved glances when Blaze finally ended the silence.

"I guess I shouldn't be surprised."

"That really should be my line, given your recent behavior," Anna replied, her mouth pulled into an unforgiving line.

"You're disappointed." It was not a question as Blaze met her eyes, the sadness in his voice palpable, causing more awkward foot-shuffling from the rest of us.

"Are you sure you want to do this here?" She nodded around the room but her eyes remained locked on Blaze, who was starting to resemble an ice sculpture fracturing under her laser-like glare. "In front of your crew?"

I gave him credit, Blaze managed to move his lips and little else.

"Hey guys, can you give us ten?" He squinted at Anna, before adding, "Make that twenty."

"You want us to step out, too?" Leah attempted to offer her—and us—one last out.

"Nope, I want you right where you are," Anna replied firmly.

"Wow, bringing in backup," Blaze commented before hacking

out a rough laugh. Noting Anna's tapping foot, he added, "Maybe I should let the crew stay. It seems like this could get dicey."

Only for tourists, I thought wryly, just as Anna responded, "Don't play me, Blaze. You know I have a black belt. And a detective's license on top of that."

The man was smart—he held his hands up in surrender.

"Decker warned me from that start, said that I should have told you."

"And yet, you didn't." Anna's angry tone didn't ease but she uncrossed her arms and opened them to him.

Blaze shook his head and started to pace. "Despite Decker's advice, I thought things would get better. Or just resolve themselves."

"You shouldn't blame her for coming to me." Leah and I nodded in agreement as Anna continued, "It'd be a shame to have her services wasted because *she* was the one who chose to do the right thing by coming to me when you wouldn't."

"I won't fire her," Blaze replied, still pacing. "She did me a favor, even though you're disappointed that you had to hear it elsewhere." Anna said nothing, permitting him no consolation, nor conceding the point. Blaze stopped, looked at her. Nodded. "All right…awkward silence." Blaze chuckled but there was no humor behind it as he elected to change the subject.

"Your boy is looking good." He nodded at Nicoh, who was absently chewing on his foot.

Though I knew it was a diversion—an attempt to diffuse some of Anna's anger—I doubted it had the effect he'd hoped.

It certainly hadn't worked on me and while I was here at Anna's request, I knew the boundaries of civility.

"Yeah, he's trimmed up a bit," I replied after a moment, keeping my tone even as I stroked the fur behind Nicoh's ears, finding myself flashing back to the recuperation period we'd both been forced to endure—under Leah's watchful eye—just a few short weeks earlier.

I knew Anna had filled Blaze in on the events that had transpired—and nearly led to our deaths—and was thankful it was not necessary to rehash the details. Nor was the timing optimal for laying out all the gory details—no matter who was doing the asking.

Apparently, Anna agreed.

"Let's be clear. I am not here on a friendly fiancé drive-by to play kissy-face. I am here to find out—from you—in nauseating detail, what's been going on so that you, I and Decker can identify and eliminate the source of this problem. Pronto." Blaze opened his mouth and closed it. Anna nodded her approval. "Yup, it's time to start talking because I'm not moving from this spot until I get exactly what I came for."

Blaze, probably realizing he had nowhere to go, jabbed a finger at her. "See, that…that there is exactly why I didn't want to involve you…or…"

"Who? Abe and Elijah?" Anna snapped.

Blaze shrugged. "It certainly seems like they've rubbed off on you."

"You didn't have any trouble reaching out to them for help when you needed a reference, despite the fact your fiancé also happens to be a licensed private detective and more than fully qualified to handle situations like this. Didn't you feel the least bit guilty about being less than honest when you told them why you needed it?" Blaze opened his mouth, immediately shutting it, causing Anna to scoff as she added, "Oh, and Sweetie Pie? Don't bother giving me that 'conflict of interest' bit, either."

Blaze chewed the inside of his mouth. I hoped he was giving the answer a decent amount of thought, otherwise, I feared Anna would unleash a bit of that black belt on him. When he finally spoke, he proceeded slowly, as though weighing the potential impact of every word.

"Like I said before, I honestly didn't want to get anyone involved until I was able to fully assess and comprehend what, or who, it was we were dealing with. Admittedly, I waited too long to do so…especially with you."

"Yeah, well, while you were off *assessing* the situation, I thought you were having an affair," Anna ground out through clenched teeth.

Blaze cocked his head. "You've got to be kidding. An affair? Really, Anna?"

"What was I supposed to think?" Anna threw her arms up. "You wouldn't talk to me and even when you did manage to show up, you weren't exactly…present." Blaze shook his head until she added, "Of course, then I saw you with her."

Blaze eyes widened in surprise and he started to speak, but then clamped his mouth shut and fidgeted with something in his pocket for a long moment before responding. "You know, Decker told me she thought you were watching us."

Anna raised an eyebrow and gestured for him to continue.

"It was after she'd caught a glimpse of you across the street when we entered that dive bar. Then, she followed you while you were following me to one of our meetings, but she didn't tell me until afterward, which is when she recommended that I bring you into the fold and let you know what had been going on."

"And yet, you *still* decided against it." Anna huffed out a breath when Blaze could do nothing but shrug. "Whatever, Blaze. We'll deal with that later. Right now, let's talk about these threats. And I do mean *right now*."

Blaze nodded. "It started a few months ago. At first, it was small things: misplaced props, faulty equipment…stuff like that. We chalked it up being tired, poor craftsmanship…whatever.

Then it moved onto what seemed like pranks but those quickly moved into accidents." He paused, pacing as he did.

"What kind of accidents?" Leah prompted. She and I had been silent for so long, both Anna and Blaze jumped. "Sorry," she mumbled.

Blaze waved her off and continued, "We thought mice were chewing through our cables but on closer inspection, several of them had been stripped with a knife or wire cutters, but we didn't realize that until after the fire."

"Fire?" Anna, Leah and I said at once, waking Nicoh and causing him to release a sharp bark as he popped into an upright position.

"Sorry, boy," Blaze murmured, bending to pat him on the head. "We thought it was nothing more than an unfortunate accident."

"It's that type of thinking that's gotten us to where you—and we—are right now," Anna replied, frowning.

Blaze blew out a breath. "True. But I can't go back now. I can only apologize for what I unintentionally put you through and ask that you forgive me." He peered at Anna, his voice pleading.

Anna stared back but sadness was replaced with hurt as tears threatened to emerge from watery eyes. Leah and I both glanced away, uncomfortable with what should have been a private moment.

She wiped the stray tears away with the back of her hand before continuing, "Decker said that these threats extended to the crew's families?"

Blaze nodded. "I'm afraid so. Again, generally speaking, they could have been isolated incidents, but when you look at then as a whole…" He looked away as his voice drifted off.

"Tell us," Anna replied, her voice firm.

"Bryce's daughter, Emily, found one of the family's cats dead on the front porch. It was bad enough, an eight-year-old having to come upon her pet dead but to find it…like that…" Again, his voice trailed off, barely a whisper.

He was quiet for so long, I thought Anna would prod him but she remained silent until he continued. "The cat had been mutilated. Bryce immediately knew it was no accident—some freak had not only put a lot of effort into gutting it, he had also staged quite a display for the family to witness."

Anna pressed her hand to her mouth. "Poor Em!"

Blaze nodded. "Sasha immediately packed up the kids—pretty much the entire house—and moved them back to her parent's summer house in Minnesota. That was two months ago."

"That explains why she hasn't returned any of my calls," Anna replied, looking at me.

I nodded, remembering that Sasha was one of Anna's bridesmaids. In her more recent phone calls, Anna had shared her concerns over Sasha's sudden lack of interest in the wedding and we'd run through possible scenarios as to why she had all but fallen off the wedding plan train—from trying to wrangle three kids to increased workload—and still Anna hadn't been able to shake the feeling something was amiss with Bryce's wife. Apparently, she had been right to worry.

"T-Dog also had his tires slashed," Blaze added.

"T-Dog?" Leah mouthed.

I could only shrug—the name was not familiar to me.

Without looking at us, Anna murmured, "Tate."

Blaze nodded and continued detailing incidents other members of the crew had encountered, each one more bizarre than the last but thankfully, not as gruesome as the scene at Bryce's house. When he finished, I noticed he had carefully avoided leaving one person's name off that list.

His.

Anna had noticed the omission as well. "What about you?"

"What do you mean?" Blaze asked, though the tightness of his tone suggested he knew exactly what direction his fiancé was heading.

"Have you or your family been on the receiving end of any threats?" Anna prodded.

He shook his head, his brow furrowing. "That's the funny thing—though funny isn't really the right word, considering, is it? Anyway, except for the site-specific events, I haven't, nor has my family, been the target of anything."

"Yet," Anna replied dryly.

Blaze nodded. "Exactly."

I glanced at Leah. Nothing like waiting for the other shoe to drop.

"I assume you've talked to your father about all of this so that he and your mother are aware and can take the necessary precautions." Anna posed no question.

Blaze glanced away. "No, I'd prefer not to get him involved. You know how he is."

Anna thrust her hand on her hip. "How, then, do you know that *this* has not affected him? Or you're mother, for goodness sake?"

"Oh, I'd think I'd know," he replied sourly. "The whole world would have heard about it."

"Damn it, Blaze! I'm not talking about hearing about it on TV. The man needs to know that there are potential threats out there. He's your family. You may not like it but you owe it to him." Blaze crossed his arms, frowning. "Could you honestly live with yourself if something happened to him…or your mother?"

"Of course not, but think about it, Anna. I could put all of us, including you, in even more danger if my father gets involved."

"So that's why you've been keeping your distance, from me….to keep your father from getting involved?" Anna raised a brow.

"I didn't say that. And I think I've already explained my oversight where you were concerned. I obviously didn't do a very good job of thinking things through," he replied.

"Oversight? That's rich, Blaze, but we'll deal with that later. In private," she gritted out. "So what does Decker think? Has she found anything? Have a line on who might be involved? Or why?"

"No on the latter but she's looked into several possibilities… lobbyists, environmentalists, businesses, sports enthusiasts, crazed and angry fans—"

"Angry fans?" I asked.

Blaze shrugged. "People who are bummed that I've stepped back from the X-sports gig."

"What—they'd prefer you go out in flames? Or die trying?" Leah asked, causing Anna to shudder. "Sorry, under the circumstances, that was not my best choice of words."

Before Blaze could respond, a crew member burst into the tent, his face red as sweat trickled down his cheeks.

"Blaze, you'd better come quick." Each word came out in a huff as he struggled to catch his breath. "There's been another accident. And this time it's bad."

"Define 'bad,' Cam," Blaze demanded, going to the man and gripping his shoulders.

Cam's body shook, his eyes wide as he stared not at, but through, Blaze. Finally, he managed to blurt out, "Bryce lost control of his bike on the PCH!"

CHAPTER SIX

If Cam hadn't been overwhelmed when he arrived, I could only imagine he was out of his gourd at the onslaught of questions being tossed at him as we raced back to the vehicles. Blaze jumped into Anna's SUV with us while Cam took the lead on his bike.

No one spoke despite the tension swirling as we traversed the nauseatingly endless path winding up the Pacific Coast Highway —its treacherous cross-backs combined with the sliver of two-lane road and sparse guardrails that divided drivers from a gut-wrenching plunge into the ocean were the only things preventing us from exceeding the speed limit.

Anna white-knuckled the steering wheel, attempting to keep pace with Cam while I gripped the armrest. Leah, typically up for any adventure, chewed her nails as Blaze worked his jaw, squinting after Cam's taillights as his friend leaned the bike into the curves, narrowly escaping the pavement's bitter kiss.

There hadn't been time to ask him for the specific location of the accident but our destination soon became clear when we were hit by a flood of lights as traffic in both directions skidded to an abrupt stop.

Blaze jumped out of the SUV before Anna could put it into park and raced toward Cam, who had already dismounted his bike and was in a full sprint, weaving in and out of cars with his friend in close pursuit, both of them ignoring the blaring horns of impatient drivers. The three of us—with Nicoh leading the pack—attempted to follow but the dark of night only aided the gridlock, blocking Cam and Blaze from view.

We had jogged more than half a mile when Anna spotted Blaze among the growing crowd of onlookers with Cam at his side.

"There!" she yelled, calling out their name, only to have her voice muffled by the chaos.

We hustled toward the pair, hoping to catch up before we lost sight of them again, watching as they pushed their way through the mass. Several people recognized Blaze and created a path so that he and Cam could pass, slapping them on the backs as they passed. Fearing we'd never catch up, Leah, Anna, and I surged forward, hoping to capitalize on the generosity they'd afforded Blaze but the gap quickly closed.

Anna surprised us both as she pulled her P.I. badge, held over her head and screamed, "Detective!"

The crowd gave her a thorough once-over but didn't give the badge itself an ounce of scrutiny—either not wanting to be involved or questioned, or fearful of repercussions—and quickly stepped aside so she could make her way through. Then again, considering the looks several of the guys were giving her, I was betting the concession had to do more with Anna herself.

Given the circumstances, I honestly didn't care one way or the other, deciding to make my own opportunity.

"We're with her!" I yelled, letting Nicoh take the lead.

His sheer size permitted us an easy opening to follow but the persistence of our little group helped create a continuous pathway to Anna as many onlookers backed away, perhaps shocked by the tenacity of our onslaught.

After several minutes, we found Blaze and Cam pressed against the barricade police had set up to cordon off looky-loos so that they could focus their attention on the rescue efforts.

As I scanned the crowd, I noticed several other members of Blaze's crew from the tent were also present, making their way to him just as he began to argue with one of the officers charged with keeping the crowd the bay. I tugged Anna's sleeve and pointed, forcing us to hasten our approach.

"You don't understand, man! That's my best friend!" Blaze gestured toward the area illuminated by the flashing lights of emergency vehicles.

"I need you to calm down, son." The officer held up a hand and when Blaze started to protest, placed it firmly against his chest. "We've got an active scene here and for the safety of every-one, I need you to remain calm and stand down."

When we reached Blaze, Anna gently touched his forearm. "Blaze, please, let them do their job. Let them help Bryce."

"Thank you, ma'am," the officer replied, nodding at her, though his eyes never diverted from Blaze, who fisted his hands and worked his jaw.

Anna interjected in an attempt to appease both parties. "We understand there was an accident involving a motorcycle." When the officer's gaze shifted from Blaze to her, she continued, "We believe a very close friend ours, Bryce Denton, may have been involved and if there's anything any of us"—she gestured to the group huddled nearby"—can do to assist…or any information we can provide…please, just ask."

The officer perused Blaze's crew and several nodded their agreement, despite the array of emotions spanning their faces—shock, fear, anguish.

"I appreciate that Miss, and I may take you up on that but right now, I'm afraid I can't tell you anything—"

"Oh, my God!" A woman screamed, interrupting whatever final commentary the officer intended to impart.

A group of firefighters and emergency personnel dispersed across the embankment as a twisted piece of metal was winched from the side of the cliff. At one time it might have resembled the frame of a motorcycle but now, it was nothing more than an unrecognizable mass of steel.

The technicians carefully heaved it over the lip of the drop before depositing it onto a trailer. The crane's release was like a pained final cry, causing me to shudder, despite the humidity of the ocean air that had already caused an unladylike amount of sweat to trickle down the back of my neck.

They repeated the process over and over, taking way too long for all of us—as the parts and pieces revealed over the crest presented no evidence of its rider.

Leah caught my eye and grasped my hand. We'd been on the receiving end of similar situations on more than one occasion. It never got easier.

Whatever the news, it wouldn't be good.

"You're surprisingly calm," she murmured as we watched Anna lean into Blaze, who wrapped an arm around her and pulled her close.

"I don't know, Leah." My grip on her hand tightened as I shook my head. "You know when they say the mind can only absorb so much before it becomes numb?"

"I do," she replied, stroking Nicoh's ears absently with her opposite hand, her tone somber.

"I'd hate to say that I was already there but—" My voice trailed off as my best friend finished my thought.

"But sometimes you've got to preserve whatever shell is left of the person you once were before fate takes over and makes you someone entirely different."

I tilted my head back and managed to hack out something that was far too harsh to have been construed as laughter.

"Well, that was a little darker and way more prophetic than I would have phrased it, but thanks for giving me the CliffNotes version of my psyche."

It was the best snark I could conjure, given the circumstances.

Leah snorted. "Yeah, if I had only been talking about *your* psyche."

I nodded.

Been there.

Done that.

I frowned, both frustrated and saddened that the drama that had recently overtaken my life had affected not only her career but her well-being. It made me wonder whether she would have been better off ditching me and my baggage altogether.

Of course, knowing me for as long as she had, Leah immediately sensed my discomfort and mock-punched my arm.

"Hey, I wouldn't change anything, bestie."

"Anything?" I asked, refusing to meet her eyes as we looked at the commotion that continued to unfold.

"We can't control the world, AJ, only our reactions to whatever it dishes out."

I nodded, blowing out a long breath.

"I just wish it would stop oozing into the lives of everyone we care about."

"Well, then we'll just have to squeeze it back into the tube, won't we?" she replied.

I snorted. "There are no bandaids in life, Leah."

Suddenly, Blaze broke free from Anna's embrace, leaped over the police barrier and charged toward the flashing lights. The officer we'd spoken to earlier took pursuit after him, yelling into the radio on his shoulder for backup. Of course, his absence left an opening for the rest of Blaze's crew and they quickly jumped the barrier, sprinting in the direction their friend had taken.

Anna was momentarily shocked but hopped over and joined the pack. I glanced at Leah, who shrugged and soon, we too, followed suit, with Nicoh taking the lead.

By the time we caught up with Blaze, he was face down on the ground with his hands cuffed behind his back. Several of his friends had found themselves in the same predicament and an angry verbal exchange had erupted as the officers attempted to keep the group under control.

"Please, sir, they are just concerned about their friend." Anna pleaded with another officer as we rushed to her side.

"They were warned to stand down on multiple occasions, many of which were issued before they decided to breach the barriers meant to keep them safe—" Anna started to interrupt, but he raised a hand. "And allow us to do our jobs."

"Can you at least tell us if you found him?" Anna asked.

"What makes you all so sure this accident involved your friend?"

"That!" Though still on his stomach, Blaze twisted his head in the direction of the trailer containing the mass of twisted metal. "That's Bryce's bike, man!"

The officer squinted at Blaze. "Are you sure he was riding it and that he didn't just lend it to someone?"

"No, man, I…talked to him…right before," Blaze replied, his voice raspy.

The officer looked at Anna. "Is that true?"

She nodded. "We saw Bryce at the beach and though we did not see him leave on the bike, it makes sense." She squinted at the officer as he blew out a long breath and looked at the bike. "Oh my, God, you know something!"

The officer surveyed her before answering, "We're still working—"

"Where is he?" Blaze interjected and once again, it took two officers to subdue him as he attempted to rise to his feet while Cam started testing the patience of his handlers. "Come on, man, you gotta let me see him!"

"You"—the officer next to us pointed at Blaze—"need to calm down or I will have my men haul all of your butts out of here. We already have enough on our plates without having to babysit a bunch of spoiled extreme sports junkies."

Blaze stopped struggling and stared at the officer, his mouth open.

"Yeah, I know who you are. A few of my guys are fans but that does not give you the right to disrupt an active scene. Got it?" The group nodded and he continued, "Anyway, as I started to say, we're still working the scene. The accident appears to have involved a single vehicle—a motorcycle."

"What about Bryce? How badly is he hurt?" Anna's tone was hopeful. "Is he conscious? Could he tell you what happened? Or how he lost control?"

"I'm betting he's pissed," one of Blaze's guys called out. "He just got that bike paid off."

The officer looked toward the cliff and blew out a long breath before facing us again. "No."

"No, he's not pissed? Or no he's not conscious?" Cam pressed.

"Neither." The officer remained stoic, his face revealing nothing more.

"Okay, so, he's not conscious," Anna replied. "That's probably to be expected, based on the damage to the bike. But how is Bryce? Surely they tended to him before messing with it? Truthfully, we're all more than curious to learn—just how bad *are* his injuries?" She prattled on, either ignoring or unaware of the lack of expression on the officer's face. "Hopefully you will allow Blaze to travel in the ambulance with him. The two have been tied at the hip since they were five and Bryce's mom caught them jumping off the roof of the garage when Blaze convinced their little band of idiots that they could fly…"

As Anna babbled, Leah and I glanced at one another, noting that the officer continued to be strangely quiet as he looked off into the distance.

Finally, he spoke, "Whoever went over the cliff, whether he was your friend or not, he's not going to be able to tell us anything anytime soon, if ever. The crew will continue their efforts but I need you to understand, we've already transitioned from rescue to recovery."

The world spun on its axis as we collectively absorbed the officer's words and the message he was taking great pains to deliver.

"Where is he? Where is Bryce?" The only thing more agonizing than the pain in Blaze's voice was the anguish that spanned his face.

"I'm sorry, sir." The officer replied, his tone even but grim.

Blaze wailed and several of his crew yelled out. This time, he broke free from his handlers and made it a dozen steps before being tackled to the ground, this time by Cam, who had also surprisingly escaped his handlers.

"There's no way he could have made it, Blaze," Cam said quietly, working to secure his friend.

"What does that mean?" Blaze thrashed as Leah and I moved to embrace Anna as she leaned into us, her thin frame shuddering.

Her voice sounded hollow. "It means Bryce is gone."

CHAPTER SEVEN

Chaos ensued as Blaze—despite being handcuffed—thrashed about and struggled to break free from his handlers. They had anticipated the movement and shoved the group in the opposite direction, just as backup arrived to escort the rowdy bunch away from the scene.

Anna stared after Blaze, her face pained as tears began streaming down her face.

"Don't worry about Blaze, we'll get him out on bail, if needed," I said, pulling her into an embrace, though I knew at the end of the day, that would be the least of her concerns.

She shook her head. "I'm not worried about him getting arrested."

I mentally kicked myself, immediately thinking that perhaps my attempt at offering comfort had translated as insensitivity. Gah —I was so bad at this.

Anna sensed my discomfort and squeezed my hand. "I simply meant that he and his guys will be released from their cuffs and sent off without as much as a stern warning—provided that they agree to leave the premises quietly." Catching Leah's frown, Anna shrugged and added, "Seriously, no one's going to want to deal with Terrence once he hears his son has been arrested.

"Best to just catch and release and call it day. No sense incurring the paperwork and the famous Edwards' migraine, especially if any of the facts turn out to be wrong. It would be a nightmare that law enforcement couldn't afford to spend the time, money or effort fighting. And it wouldn't go away quietly." Anna paused to shake her head. "I'm more concerned about Blaze's state of mind once they find Bryce and bring his body home."

"Why don't we get you out of here?" I suggested. "Once we get back, we'll track Blaze down so that the two of you can talk and take care of whatever....after."

She squeezed my arm. "I appreciate that. I'd like to find out more about the accident so that I can help Blaze and the others deal with what's likely to come, but I'm still determined to identify whoever's behind the threats," she glanced at the accident site before adding, "even though the timing feels a bit inappropriate."

"I know what you mean," I replied, having been there. "With everyone's guard down, this might actually be the ideal time to keep pushing forward."

Anna nodded. "That's exactly what I was thinking. And also what worries me."

"We're here to help." After Leah concurred by giving Anna a thumbs-up, I added, "You need to be with Blaze. So tell us, what can we do?"

"You're right." Anna sighed, finally turning away from the scene to face us. "Perhaps while I check on Blaze, you could help me track Decker down. I want to find more about the threats and what conclusions she's formed—or insights she's gleaned— through the course of her investigation."

"Done," Leah replied.

Anna and I squinted in confusion as Leah nodded in the opposite direction. Decker strode purposefully toward us, a healthy frown covering her face.

"I heard," she said calmly once she reached us and looked from face to face, her mouth pulled into a firm line as she surveyed the activity over our shoulders.

"You talked to Blaze?" Anna asked.

Decker shook her head. "Saw him at a distance. Cops were giving him and the crew a severe tongue-lashing as they uncuffed them and placed them into cruisers."

"I thought you said they wouldn't be arrested." Leah looked at Anna, who shrugged, equally perplexed.

"They weren't. Arrested, that is," Decker replied. "Police wanted them out of their way—meaning out of view of the investigation—and the only way they could ensure that happened is if they escorted them off the premises. They'll probably be dropping them all off at their respective homes and giving each a few words of warning in the process." She scoffed. "Boys are getting off easy, in my book. I would've let them stew in a cell. It would have served them right after acting like spoiled brats and impeding an investigation, not to mention endangering the lives of others, including the emergency personnel just trying to do their jobs."

"Their friend is still out there somewhere. Probably dead," Anna replied dryly. "Not everyone is made of stone."

"Touché," Decker replied, never blinking an eye as she and Anna attempted to stare the other down.

Leah gave me a sideways glance before interjecting, "Err, it was probably not a bad idea—I doubt anyone was in a condition to drive. I know I wouldn't have been."

"Me either," I added.

Anna nodded and her shoulders relaxed a bit, though her hands were still firmly pressed against her hips and her stance was rigid. "If Blaze didn't tell you about the accident, how did you know?"

Decker worked her jaw. "Cop friend spotted me and gave me the low-down."

"Huh, mighty nice cop friend," Anna replied, gritting her teeth. "Didn't think they were supposed to divulge information to average citizens—certainly not while they're in the middle of working an active scene."

Decker shrugged. "His pops was friends with mine. They went way back. And, not that it makes me any more than average, but the two of us also grew up in the same neighborhood. Then again, I might have also reminded him that I'd kicked his skinny butt on more than one occasion when we were in grade school."

She shrugged when the three of us raised our brows. "What can I say, I took offense when he tried to kiss me and put him in his place. On the ground. He went home and cried to his mama, though I didn't hurt him all that bad. Anyway, now that he's a big bad cop, it never hurts to dangle that nugget of history out there whenever it suits. Today, I felt as though it was warranted."

"So you played one of your cards," I replied.

She offered me a wry smile, which translated into a cruel curl at the corner of her mouth. "Let's just say I hold the whole deck."

"Okay, you saw Blaze, Cam and the others, but how did you know we were here?" Anna asked.

Decker pointed at Nicoh, who sat at attention. "He's hard not to notice. My friend zeroed in on you when you arrived and described this big guy to a T."

She stooped to scruff Nicoh under the chin and was rewarded a whoo-woo of approval.

Anna frowned. "So, if he saw us arrive, he also saw us breach the police barrier. And still, he let us follow Blaze. What gives?"

"I don't disagree with your assessment," Decker replied, her expression revealing nothing.

I shook my head. I really hated it when people took that tack. You either agree. Or you don't. It reminded me of my days in my high school math class—which I sucked at—where I struggled to remember that a negative and a negative made a positive. Or was it a negative? Whatever, it was a half-baked response and Decker was smart enough to realize it the minute she spewed it out.

Of course, she caught my look and smirked before turning toward Anna.

"Peedy had enough problems to contend with as it was but yeah, he sent word on ahead. One of the other cops recognized Anna as Blaze's girlfriend and figured the three—four—of you wouldn't escalate the situation with Blaze and his pals. In fact, they agreed that you might come in handy to get the boys out of there without creating more of a distraction."

"Peedy?" We all asked in unison.

"Officer Piedmont. My friend and one of the most loyal and honorable people I've ever known. And I'm just not saying that because I've seen him in his tighty-whiteys when we were kids. He's also a dedicated and hard-working law enforcement professional who knows how to judge a situation."

Anna refocused the conversation, her tone laden with bitterness. "Yeah, well, I guess that was a big fail on our part, allowing things to get out of hand, that is."

"Don't be too hard on yourselves. It was on law enforcement to make the call. And they did," Decker replied, surveying us one by one. "And in case you were wondering, which by the looks on your faces you are, Peedy wasn't the only who saw you breach the police barrier, even it if was to follow Blaze. I would have done the same, if it matters at all. Then again, given what I've just told you, you're probably not all that surprised." She snorted after taking in our expression.

"Anyway, I'm just saying it was their choice to make. They let you stay and despite the fact they had to take Blaze and his pals down, cuff all of them and expend valuable time and energy on it, that's on them—and on Blaze and his friends for acting out. To your credit, you guys certainly didn't make the same choice to engage the offices and therefore did not make the situation any worse."

It was a small concession, I guessed. And in hindsight, Decker hadn't needed to put it out there and yet, she had.

Because she needed us—for whatever *that* was worth.

Anna sighed wearily. "So, this cop friend, did he have anything else to share?"

Decker nodded. "He did, which is why I wanted to find you. I need your help."

"Again?" Anna huffed and crossed her arms when Decker shrugged. "You are something else. You know that, right?" She didn't wait for a response before adding, "Enlighten us. Do you need help with this—or with your investigation of the threats?"

"Both," Decker replied. "They could very well be one and the same."

Anna shook her head. "Sorry, I'm wiped out but still, I'm not sure I'm following. Exactly what insights did your officer friend have to offer?"

Decker frowned but replied, "Well, obviously they're not going to confirm this was anything more than a horrible accident until they locate Bryce and the Medical Examiner releases an official report, but Peedy did reveal something interesting regarding the circumstances of the accident itself. Off the record, of course."

"Yeah yeah, we know the drill." Leah rolled her eyes as she waved a hand, urging Decker to move it along.

"Okay, first oddity, there were no skid marks."

"Sure, which suggests Bryce might have been going too fast and didn't have enough time to brake. Not that surprising, given the cutbacks and the cliffs," Anna replied.

"Yeah, plus when Bryce left, he was in a...mood," Leah added. "He and Blaze had just gone at it."

Decker shrugged. "Interesting, but perhaps not all that relevant."

"How could it not be relevant?" Leah asked, waving her hands. "Bryce was clearly pissed when he stormed off and made no bones about wanting to get the hell away from Blaze. He certainly needed to blow off some steam, at the very least. Having said that, he could have hopped on his bike, laid on the gas and used the open road to get lost in his thoughts. Meaning, he could have been so distracted that he may not have realized how fast he was going until it was too late." She paused to take a breath. "Then again, maybe he saw the curves as a challenge—"

"Any portion of that may have been true but it wouldn't have mattered," Decker replied somberly. "None of it would have done him any good in the end."

"Come again?" Leah asked.

Decker blew out a long breath before responding, "Even if Bryce had been traveling at a normal rate of speed and used his brakes rounding the curves, they wouldn't have worked when he needed them."

"What? Why?" The three of us responded in tandem.

"Because someone made sure he wouldn't be able to stop," Decker replied.

"What are you saying?" Anna pressed a hand to her mouth.

"Someone had manipulated various parts on his bike. Even the slightest adjustment could have caused any number of scenarios to occur once the pressure of the vehicle on the pavement was combined with speed—his wheels could have come loose, his brakes may not have engaged, the gas could have cut out—regardless, the outcome would have been the same."

"Sabotage," I whispered.

Decker frowned. "More than sabotage."

I reflected on the image of the bike as it was hoisted over the cliff and how it had been turned into nothing more than scrap metal, rising over the cliff. "Certain death."

"Another threat," Anna murmured.

"Only this time, they called Blaze's bluff," Decker replied, not caring about the harshness of her phrasing.

"I can't stand this." Anna began moving toward the direction where we'd parked. "I need to get to Blaze."

"Are you sure you're okay to drive?" Leah called after her but Anna hastened her pace.

"I am. And after I find my fiancé and make sure he's in one piece, I'm going after the person…or people….who started this." Anna's reply came out more of a growl, causing the three of us to look at one another in surprise as we stared at her back while she trudged forward.

I didn't blame her for her reaction, but it was a side of my friend I hadn't seen before. It wasn't as though I'd expected her to fall apart, but this was a darkness that I would have never seen coming if it wasn't standing directly in front of me, smacking me in the face.

Fortunately, Decker stepped in, matching Anna stride for stride. "Why don't I give them a ride back? You go to Blaze and I'll fill these two in on what I know. Then we'll all meet up and get a fresh start in the morning and come up with a game plan to divide and conquer."

"Sounds good to me," Anna replied, pausing briefly to glance at us for approval.

Leah and I nodded and gave her a hug before she blew out a long breath and jumped into her SUV. We watched as she quickly flipped a U-turn and headed back in the direction we'd originally come.

"I'm over there." Decker pointed.

For a moment, I hoped we wouldn't be traveling all the way

back to L.A. crammed into a sidecar and was pleasantly surprised when she directed us to a newer-model Range Rover.

Decker noticed our open mouths and snickered. "I think you'll be comfortable in this. Your boy, Nicoh, will have a good amount of space to stretch his legs. In fact, I think there are probably some dog treats back there for him, if not a nylon bone to keep him busy during our trip back to the city."

I worked my mouth, formulating the appropriate words, and finally managed to sputter out, "Figured you as more of a Harley gal, Decker."

She tossed her head back and released her version of a laugh, a cross between a snort and a hack. "Actually, I am. This is my work vehicle." She opened the rear passenger door and urged Nicoh in.

He sniffed the interior before jumping in, finding a space to spread out before releasing a low moan of approval when he found the bone.

"You have a dog?" I asked as I jumped in the back with Nicoh and Leah took the front passenger seat.

"Don't sound so shocked. Yeah, she's with a friend right now. Figured she didn't need all the excitement."

I nodded. "What's her name?"

"Mia. She's almost ten. A retired police dog. She has her days, suffers from arthritis in her back legs and hips, so I try not to get her all worked up. Other days, she surprises me and goes all puppy crazy. Really likes the water."

"That's cool. I hear swimming can be therapeutic for animals," I replied, continuing when Decker nodded. "Think she'll be up to meeting Nicoh? He doesn't have anywhere near the skill set she does but he's been trained and he's very good with other dogs."

"Sure, when the time is right, why don't we schedule a meet

and greet and see how it goes," Decker replied, sounding genuinely interested.

"Yeah, when we figure this all out," I replied. "And in case you were wondering, Leah and I are not leaving until we do."

"Definitely," Leah replied, before adding, "I'm curious about something, Decker. It seemed as though you weren't all that disappointed when Anna went after Blaze alone. Was that your original intent—to get us by ourselves—to pick our brains?"

Decker laughed at Leah's assessment. "Forgot you used to be an investigative reporter, Campbell, and a good one, from what I've heard."

I chuckled when Leah blushed. It was the second time Decker had called her number.

"Just to be clear, I have no bones with Anna Goodwin, though I can understand her animosity toward me, given the circumstances," Decker replied.

I believed her. "Anna will come around. We just need to look at things from her perspective. For months, she's been trying to figure out what's going on in her relationship. Blaze should have known that she would understand and should have realized she'd think she'd done something wrong when he didn't come clean. Just look at her. She's exhausted, rundown and barely able to keep herself upright. It's not surprising that she used all of her free time trying to figure out what was going on…and then once she did, who could blame her?"

I raised my hand when Decker started to comment. "She's not angry with you, specifically. She's raging about the situation and how it went down. She's probably a little humiliated, too, that she didn't see things for what they were. I guess what I'm saying is, Anna's beef—and she knows it—is with Blaze, and not you." Decker's frown was clearly visible as she stared at me from the rearview mirror. "Come on, Decker, you know it's true. You may not know Anna, but you know people. And right now, you need allies to help you figure this out. I am telling you, straight up, you can count on Anna."

Decker gave me a single head nod. "Fair enough. And, if we're being completely frank here, you Phoenix chicks are a surprise. A refreshing one. I've read your dossiers and then some"—she paused to give me a wry smile—"and I know what you're both capable of…and what you've already been through."

I noted she didn't mention the similarities in our backgrounds, having lost loved ones to murder, though she quickly added, "And believe me, I don't say this lightly—I both admire and respect who you are and what you stand for. And what you stand against. Which is why, as Anna's friends, I'd like to pick your brains. And, before you ask, yes, I'm willing to exchange deets on the flip side but before I do, I want to get a sense of Blaze and Anna's relationship—from your perspectives—and the relationship between Anna and Blaze and his friend Bryce before I shared my initial findings with her."

"You're afraid that she'll deny there's any truth to it?" Leah asked.

"I am," Decker replied. "Before Bryce's accident, I told Blaze I had a line on a possible culprit behind the threats. Of course, it makes zero sense, given everything that's happened today but at the time, I had evidence that clearly implicated one person—for everything."

"Well, don't just leave us hanging, Decker." Leah's tone suggested she was less than amused, if not impatient.

Decker shook her head. "I'm afraid I'm the only one left out hanging. I should have never revealed my suspicions until I'd confirmed every piece of evidence. Now, I feel as though I set something in motion…something that I can never take back…" Her voice broke but when I surveyed her reflection, her face revealed nothing.

"No judgment here, Decker, just tell us what you found," I replied quietly. "And why you think you are the catalyst."

"Because, shortly before Bryce went off that cliff, I convinced Blaze that his best friend was hell-bent on destroying the life—and the only world—he had ever known."

CHAPTER EIGHT

"What? Whoa!" Leah sucked in a breath, her eyes wide as she turned to Decker. "You think that Blaze confronted him, based on your findings. And *that's* what they were arguing about?"

"I guarantee it," Decker replied somberly. "When I last talked to Blaze, I told him about the evidence and was on my way to show him proof, when…this occurred."

"You must have presented a convincing argument," I replied, careful to keep the judgment out of my tone. "And Blaze—being Blaze—couldn't contain his disappointment or hide his emotions from his childhood friend."

"I'm assuming so." Decker's voice was barely above a whisper. "Then there was the other thing."

"What *other* thing?" I asked, hoping Anna hadn't been on the mark about there being an affair.

Decker's vibe, combined with the severity of her frown, suggested it was something else altogether. When her shoulders fell, I latched onto it—regret.

"When Blaze hired me, he didn't know what he was dealing with. Didn't know who to trust. Was completely out of his gourd with paranoia. Crap, at one point, I had to convince him that Anna and the Stantons were in the clear and not suspects themselves. Honestly, I think it had to do with his upbringing and that family of his—especially his father. That man—" She shook her head. "He was so distrusting that—against my better judgment—I suggested that he put me on his crew, undercover. He was up for trying anything at that point and agreed to hire me as a production assistant."

"Didn't the others find that strange? You weren't even part of the original team," Leah commented.

"Yeah, but Blaze and I hashed out everything beforehand. Anticipated every question. We doctored up enough of a background for me that the Pentagon would have been convinced but at the end of the day, it was simply his word, and their trust in it, that sealed the deal. He convinced everyone that it was a new era. New project. New genre. Which also meant fresh perspectives.

"Ultimately, the guys just wanted to ensure that Blaze was protected. Many of them had been with him from the start and they inherently distrusted outsiders. And, after what's been going on for the past several months, I can't say I blame them. I want Blaze protected, too.

"Anyway, the more I looked into the threats—dissected them one by one—the more it started looking like an inside job. And, when it came right down to it, it also became clear that they could have been initiated and implemented by only two people. The first being Blaze himself, which would have meant he had been basically lying to me from the start. So, for the time-being, I placed that one on the back burner. The second possibility was Bryce, his best friend.

"After further inspection of his finances, I learned Bryce was over-leveraged. And I don't mean a second mortgage and high credit card debt type of leveraged. That could have been explained away. There were also dozens of outstanding medical bills from the antics he and Blaze had accumulated while filming their extreme sports videos.

"In the crew's heyday, Blaze was the one who had received the bulk of the endorsements, as he was considered the name and face of their brand. Most of the others, including Bryce, followed along just to experience the vibe and chase the next adrenaline rush. Blaze came from money and though he never accepted or relied upon it, it was a safety net he could have fallen back on, had he needed to.

"The others were just surfer dudes from the valley. Most of them never graduated from high school, while the others barely squeaked their way out. Sure, some got scholarships. Cam, for example, is actually a stellar soccer player. Bryce was decent at football but never really applied himself and fell into the skateboarding and surfing crowd, preferring to ditch practice in order to catch the serious waves. That's how he met Blaze, back when Blaze was just an extreme sports junkie with a camcorder, jumping off bridges, free-forming off cliffs, stunts like that. Bryce couldn't help but be drawn to the allure of that lifestyle.

"Don't get me wrong, Bryce was a decent guy—he and Blaze acted so much like brothers that most people thought they were cut from the same cloth—but when your back's against the wall and you have to go home and admit to your wife that the payday isn't going to come? That the kids are going to have to be pulled from their private schools and life isn't quite the ride he'd sold her on? It's a gnarly pill to swallow, especially for an aging x-sports dude who'd seen the last of his best days on the circuit."

"Hold up, Decker," Leah interjected. "You truly believed the man mutilated a pet and terrorized his own family to the point they were forced move halfway across the country?"

Decker shrugged. "I just went where the evidence took me."

Leah glanced back at me, scrunching her nose. Like the evidence never lied. "Explain."

Decker puffed her cheeks like a balloon, slowly releasing the air before responding. "Okay. Let's say we overlook the bank books and the bills that were continually piling up. I tracked down loan sharks who admitted he'd been doing a significant amount of gambling and when that didn't pay off, his line of credit was immediately cut and the debt came due.

"Like I said, at the core of his bones, Bryce was a good guy but he didn't want to face reality or man-up and take ownership of his failures. Not to himself. Not to his family. And certainly not to Blaze. That, and he'd probably played way too many video games or watched too many action movies. He was good at what he did but also did some really stupid stuff. Case in point: I found evidence in his garage that corroborated his involvement in the threats." Decker paused to laugh but there was no humor behind it, shaking her head. "Really stupid, incriminating evidence."

"You broke into his garage?" I asked.

Decker snorted. "You can't break into something that was left wide open." I shook my head, casting a frown into the rearview mirror. Based upon her smug return, my judgment was not lost on her. "Let's just say that I knew—no matter how—that his wife had been on his case about fixing the broken garage door, which had been stuck in the open position for months.

"She was equally pissed that he refused to clean the garage, claiming the broken door allowed the entire neighborhood to bear witness to their dirty laundry. Anyway, when she moved back home with her folks, I just happened to be in the neighborhood and decided to stop by Bryce's for a quick hello. As luck would have it, he wasn't home."

Leah snorted. "You don't really strike me as the welcome wagon type."

Decker smirked at the sarcasm but shrugged. "Whatever. A neighborhood cat could have gone in and pissed on it all. The garage was left open to the public. And it told quite the story. For every threat Blaze and his guys received, there was a piece of evidence in there that linked directly back to Bryce."

"Such as?" Leah prompted.

Decker shook her head. "No offense but I'd prefer to keep the specifics to myself, for now." Before we could protest, she added, "It's not a matter of trust. It's for your own safety—the fewer people who know—the better."

"That's an interesting point. What if the perp knew the same things you did about Bryce and realized he could be an easy patsy?" I asked.

She nodded. "That could very well be true. And until a couple of hours ago, he had me convinced."

Something else was nagging at me. If Bryce had hidden his financial situation from his family, he may have been embarrassed to discuss it with his closest friends.

"What if you were right, Decker? What if Bryce knew the jig was up and when Blaze confronted him—"

"And he purposely plunged off that cliff?" Decker shook her head. "I don't see it. He may have let his family down in the past, but he wouldn't have left them with nothing."

"How could he even get a life insurance policy, considering the risks associated with his choice of career?" Leah asked.

"I have no idea," Decker replied, frowning as she added, "but somehow he managed to get a fat daddy of one. And recently."

"That *is* interesting—what if that was a nugget you were privy to that the perp wasn't?" I wondered, realizing after-the-fact that I'd sputtered it out loud.

"Yeah, well, I have friends in high places." Decker managed to pull that response off without sounding conceited. It was, to her, just a matter of fact. "Then again, he may have had the information but deemed it irrelevant."

"Or just didn't care," Leah replied.

"Exactly." Decker nodded.

"Perhaps we should be more concerned with where he plans to go from here." I hated to admit it but considering the players—and the transition from random threats to mutilation to premeditated murder—the odds had not only shifted, they were currently in his favor. And while Decker may have had her resources, it was quite clear he had a few tricks in his bag, too.

"There's one other thing I should probably mention."

This time, I sensed a bit of apprehension from Decker as she white-knuckled the steering wheel. I glanced at Leah but we both remained silent until she continued.

"Blaze recently revealed—actually right before I told him about my suspicions—that Bryce had drawn the same conclusion Anna had—that Blaze was having an affair, with me." She let out a harsh laugh. "Whatever he and Anna saw, or thought they saw, we must have been way too convincing."

I nodded absently. Decker was right, it would have almost been comical, had things not turned out as they had. So much devastation—families, relationships, lives.

"Was Bryce above threatening to reveal what he knew to Anna?" Leah asked.

"You know how guys are—always giving each other crap about something." She paused, her brow creasing. "Now that you mention it, I do remember one particular snark Bryce dished out, something about watching his p's and q's with the hired help. Now, putting it into perspective, Bryce could have easily meant me."

"Do you think Blaze told Bryce who you were and why you were there during their confrontation?" I asked.

"Possibly. When I told Blaze my suspicions about Bryce, he got pretty revved up, told me I was wrong and even called me out when I outlined everything for him. I told him I would handle the confrontation with Bryce if he preferred but he said no, that he would deal with it—almost blamed himself for having the investigation turn out like it had." Decker shook her head. "Perhaps he felt guilty about what had been sitting in front of him all along."

We shook our heads but we understood the bonds, aware of the strain that secrets—no matter the reason—placed on those bonds. We'd definitely been there and done that.

Leah reached back and gripped my hand and we sat there like that for a moment before any of us spoke.

Finally, I broke the silence. "In my experience, you can't see something that's been carefully, intentionally hidden. Something, whether tangible or emotional, that someone doesn't want you to see. Sometimes it doesn't matter how strong you think the bond is or what it can endure."

"Sounds like you know a thing or two about it and can understand where Blaze was coming from," Decker replied.

"Yeah, I think both of us have certainly had our share—and fill—of secrets," I murmured, as Leah squeezed my hand harder.

As of late, our lives had been filled with them, as they continually oozed into and negatively impacted everyone we cared about. And after my last go-around, I wasn't sure I was up for another shift on the ice. I would rather get smacked in the face with a puck than lose one more person. Right now, I was clasping hands with one of the few I had left.

I released Leah's hand and swatted at the annoying moisture that threatened the corner of my eye but not before Decker caught my reflection. She held my gaze and as I'd come to expect, her expression was undecipherable as she returned her focus the road.

Leah caught the exchange and casually shifted the discussion. "We understand why Blaze wanted to address your findings with Bryce personally. Maybe it was his way of letting Bryce come clean in private, though perhaps Bryce saw it as a betrayal of their friendship."

Decker frowned. "Unfortunately, based on what you witnessed at the beach, I'm assuming that is exactly what happened. He probably called Bryce out, if not fired him, and outed me at the same time. Then again, assumption…"

"You seriously need to let that go, Decker," Leah huffed out. "You did your job and all three of us have been around the block enough to realize this jerk is acting out of something we can't even begin to understand."

Decker focused intently—too intently—on driving. Something was clearly bothering her.

"Were you trying to avoid Blaze at the crash site? Or making sure he avoided seeing you?" My questions had the desired effect, as her eyes flashed to the rearview mirror.

"I don't hide from anything," she replied. "Or anyone."

Leah tapped her chin. "You may not have done so consciously, but it certainly wouldn't have helped matters, if Blaze had realized you were at the scene. You've already encountered Anna's reaction and she hadn't even been in on confronting Bryce."

"No, I suppose not."

Something else occurred to me. "Do you think the real perp suspected, or even knew, who you were and led you down the path he wanted you to go? To ensure this was the outcome?"

Decker shrugged. "Anything's possible at this point, but the question is…why? What would have been the point?" She thrummed her fingers against the steering wheel, before adding, "Let's say you're on the right track and I'd gathered all the crumbs he laid out for me, exactly the *way* he wanted me to, *when* he wanted me to. And then, I was able put all the parts and pieces together in the timeframe he needed me to in order to make it appear as though Bryce was responsible for everything—knowing that once I did, I would immediately report my findings to Blaze —it means he would have also researched their relationship thoroughly enough to know Blaze would insist on confronting his friend directly.

"And upon being wrongly accused, that Bryce would have reacted the way he would—storming away and jumping on his bike so that he could get away from the situation and blow off steam." Decker paused to catch her breath, then added, "Which means the perp was prepared to fabricate a suicide, playing to the fact that after being confronted by his best friend, Bryce wasn't about to become a caged animal and elected the only other option in his toolkit.

"Having said that, wouldn't the threats theoretically stop, once the police ruled it as a suicide?"

"If we're talking about a rational, sane individual…sure," Leah replied.

Decker shook her head. "Then, I ask again…why? Why did they do it? I seriously doubt all of this was about making Blaze suffer for his best friend's death, which will most definitely not be ruled as a suicide, if faking a suicide was even what they had originally intended."

"If it was, it means they weren't aware of Bryce's recent life insurance policy, or the suicide clause," I added. "As you mentioned, there was no way Bryce would have left his family high and dry. And though I didn't know the man personally, based on the company he kept and the reactions everyone had, it seems unlikely he would have willingly left his family, much less used suicide as a way to escape his problems, especially if he'd done nothing illegal."

"Perhaps the perp's original intention was to slow the production down," Leah offered.

"Okay, I get that, but if this is all about the project itself, even if a crew member's death slowed Blaze down—made him rethink his priorities or put production on the back burner—it only was only a temporary fix for the perp. In the end, it raises another problem…once Bryce is found and his death ruled a homicide, he would also be cleared as the perpetrator of the threats."

I was glad that Decker was open to our style of banter—tossing random ideas back and forth—without getting all bunched up about marking her territory or needing to place blame or judgment. Honestly, time was not our friend and to be frank, she had been the one asking for the audience and should have had the cajones to understand that we were genuinely there willing to help and offer assistance, no matter how limited, to help our friend, Anna.

She nodded at my assessment. "Absolutely, which also means the investigators will likely start looking elsewhere once law enforcement wraps up their investigation of the accident site. Within a matter of days, they will start looking for the 'why' and the 'who,' if they haven't already."

"The cops will certainly want to talk to you, Decker, especially after Blaze shares his version of things. And once they sift through the evidence that led you to believe it was Bryce, they'll focus their attention on other possible suspects." I paused, before adding, "We need to be one step ahead, because the person or persons responsible have already anticipated this and have the means to go underground until the circus surrounding it dies down. We need to use this time to catch up with them, figure out their end game and head them off before they make their presence felt again. At the end of the day, they may have temporarily whet their appetite but they're nowhere near finishing the meal."

Leah nodded. "Let's start with the evidence framing Bryce and work our way back. How did they get access to the information? Why did they need a scapegoat that was on the inside and/or why did they select Bryce? Is it business? Or personal? A way to get back at Blaze for something—something that we haven't addressed yet? Because AJ is right, whatever their end game, they haven't reached it and for as far as they've already been willing to go, they are not about to stop now. They'll just redirect their efforts."

"Or start changing the rules of the game," I replied.

The perp may have made one crucial error with Bryce and even though we were stronger in numbers now, our defense would not be able to fight an offense that we couldn't see coming.

"Then, like you suggested, we need to figure out who is behind this," she replied.

Leah and I nodded.

Once we figured out 'who,' hopefully, the 'why' would fall into place.

CHAPTER NINE

"Like they say—no time like the present to get started." Leah sounded almost gleeful as she dramatically pulled her trusty notepad and pen from her tote and flipped to a blank page.

At the top she wrote "Potential Baddies" in large block lettering, causing Decker to release not one, but two snorts.

Leah's eyes never left the page as she replied, "That's right, Buttercup, time to give it up. And though it *should* go without saying, both AJ and I plan on proceeding without judgment or placing blame where you're concerned. So if you're feeling squishy, it's time for you to get over yourself already. Capiche?"

Decker chuckled and nodded. "You know, I may have underestimated the two of you and I apologize. I had you figured for a couple of Nancy Drew wannabe's, going off half-cocked without thinking things through, figuring it was better to ask for forgiveness than permission and not caring whether you got either. But considering you were able to take the bad guys down and get justice for those who deserved it, I can't fault your methods. You've certainly got moxie."

"Yeah, well, looks can be deceiving. Kind of like crap first impressions," was my best friend's response.

Though I shot her a belated grimace, I'll admit, it was well-played.

Decker looked at Leah, then at me in the rearview, before she threw her head back and released a hack of a laugh. "Good answer."

Leah pressed her lips together and looked away in an attempt to hide the pinkening of her cheeks, as both of us realized we'd dodged a bullet. The method behind our madness was safe. For now.

After taking a moment to collect herself, she tapped the pen against the pad. Too hard.

"Okay. Let's start from the beginning. Give us your gut feelings on everyone and everything, no matter how inconsequential anything seemed at the time."

Decker squinted at her. "You were pretty good at this investigative reporting stuff, huh?"

"I was the best," Leah replied without a hint of ego or attitude in her tone.

I nodded at Decker. It was simply a statement of fact.

Decker returned her focus to the highway. "Hmm…seems like you miss it—despite the parallels of doing research for the Stantons—you think you'll ever go back?"

Leah shook her head once and looked out the side window before she released a small shudder, a lingering side-effect of being kidnapped and nearly killed during her last months as a reporter covering the crime beat for a newspaper back in Phoenix.

"That one's on me Decker," I replied, saving my BFF from having to explain.

What had happened to her had, in fact, been my fault. Or, more accurately, she had been used as a tool to draw me in and kill me.

And while we'd both survived the ordeal physically, the

emotional and psychological damage still lingered, a constant reminder that our lives would never be the same.

Decker glanced speculatively from me to Leah, who continued staring out the window as she replied, "Can we get on with it already? I'd dispute my best friend's comment but I'm starting to feel as though we're gonna end up on that list of yours if we continue down this path. And for the record, returning to my old stomping ground is not on the horizon and I'd prefer to leave it at that."

Decker shrugged. "Okay, you ask, I'll answer honestly and won't bother withholding my opinion or my mouth for present company. So let's get to it, Campbell."

Leah offered a single head nod. "First, I'd like to review your initial list of possible suspects, no matter how much of a long shot they seemed."

Decker laid out her possibilities, which Leah promptly scribbled down. The first broad stroke included overzealous fans, disgruntled former employees, current crew members, environmentalists, politicians, zoning commissioners, real estate investors and on and on.. And while Decker had good reason to zone in on Bryce, she also hadn't previously found evidence suggesting any of the other candidates would have gone to the lengths the perp had to threaten Blaze and his crew.

"The fans you mentioned, I assume they were primarily enthusiasts of Blaze's extreme sports films?" I asked and when Decker nodded, added, "Could any of them have harbored enough resentment or anger when Blaze threw in the towel to do something like this?"

"Nah, for the most part, they're a pretty peaceful bunch, despite what they do and the way they do it. Blaze earned a lot of respect among his peers and fans, always offering advice and pointers to the up and comers, hanging with and chatting up the fans, any time of day or night.

"He was also forthcoming on social media, in interviews and in person about his intent on retiring by his thirtieth birthday—which he did—so there shouldn't have been any surprise there. Besides, even if a handful of zealots had been upset, they wouldn't have resorted to this. It's just not the way they roll."

"What about the current project? Is there anyone that would benefit if the film weren't made, such as residents in the community?" Leah asked.

"The residents would actually benefit from the film, if it helped ensure their beaches and livelihood weren't destroyed merely for the benefit of development," Decker replied.

"What about the potential real estate investors?" I suggested.

Decker shook her head. "The proposed beach preservation law was gaining momentum and while they tried, there was nothing they could do to stop it, especially when Blaze's film was destined to draw more attention to the issue." She paused before adding, "The goal of Blaze's film from day one has always been to generate awareness."

"Still, they couldn't have been pleased when they found about his current passion project," Leah replied. "It may not have affected them with regards to this beach and community but it does pose potential roadblocks in the future."

I nodded. "Leah's right. Once the movie is out there, other beach communities may become inspired to pursue the same conservation provision to ensure their own beach fronts and wildlife are preserved, which would make it even more difficult for investors to gobble them up for development."

"True, but wouldn't they tackle it from another angle? Maybe even try to make a case that they're proponents of boosting an economy in an area that had previously been struggling?" Decker countered. "Or, these guys could also attempt to make a case that the film production, just by being there, could be causing just as much of a disruption to the natural ecosystem, calling it a form of pollution…whatever, allowing the ecologists and conservationists to do the work for them?"

When both Leah and I shrugged, she added, "Of course, there are always other ways these investors could turn the situation into a win, especially if they appealed to Terrence Edwards and were able to gain his support."

I nodded, understanding her concern. "What about Blaze's family…his father, to be specific? According to Anna, their relationship is pretty fractured. She also mentioned he wasn't terribly thrilled about any of Blaze's previous choice of careers—I think the terms 'buffoonery' and 'schoolboy shenanigans' were tossed in there. How does he feel about this new venture of Blaze's?"

Decker snorted. "*Terry* absolutely loathes it. Thinks it's a waste of time and just another ploy Blaze fabricated in order to thumb his nose at the family name."

"Is he, Blaze that is…snubbing his family?" I asked, though I was pretty sure I knew the answer.

"Gawd, no. If anything, he's doing it to prove that he can make his own success…in a way that puts his family name in a positive light, as opposed to the way his old man tends to favor," Decker replied, shaking her head. "No, Blaze wouldn't snub his family nor would he consider taking anything from his father's wallet—which annoys Terry even more."

She paused, frowning as she added, "You know, there's not much that Blaze fears in life, but aligning with his father, or being seen in the same light, scares him more than his own mortality. And just between the three of us—I think Blaze believes his father is Lucifer himself."

"I can't imagine what growing up in a family like that must have been like. It must be even more challenging for him now, as an adult," Leah replied, scrunching her nose. "I can hardly blame Blaze for wanting to separate himself from his father."

I remembered that when Anna had hooked up with Blaze,

Leah had spent quite a bit of time researching him and his notorious family and while she found Blaze to be the real deal, she uncovered several questionable business dealings where his father was concerned.

Many of Terrence Edwards' associates had come by their money in a less than honest way and had made no bones about working outside the confines of the law to get precisely what they wanted, when they wanted it—taking it from whoever they wanted. And if there was ever any recourse, Blaze's father was there to appease the judge or law enforcement official. Those who refused to comply were often subjected to an unfortunate outcome and while it never ended in anyone's death, given their circumstances after crossing Edwards' path, it might have been preferable.

I shuddered, just as Decker added, "Could you imagine Blaze, standing side by side with old man, serving as a criminal defense attorney—sizing up potential clients during a martini lunch, wearing a three-piece suit and tie with his hair tamed and shoes polished off with a nice buff and shine?"

She released a snort after taking in my overt gagging gesture.

Leah looked equally disgusted but added, "Do you think he's above sicking his minions or his 'friends' on Blaze?" She used finger quotes on the latter.

"He does have relationships with some pretty interesting people," I replied.

"Blaze said no," Decker replied, frowning.

"But you're not so sure, are you?" I countered.

Decker shrugged. "Maybe. But at the risk of Blaze getting hurt or worse? That would be cold—even for Terry."

"Then let's approach this from another angle," Leah replied. "What about someone trying to get at his father…through Blaze?"

Decker nodded. "It's a possibility that I think we may want to look into, but…"

"But what?" Leah prodded.

"Blaze was adamant that I not engage him."

Leah snorted. "Yeah…well, once he hears about the latest regarding his son's best friend, Terrence Edwards may very well seek *us* out."

Decker released a breath before responding, "That's what I'm afraid of."

CHAPTER TEN

I changed the subject. "What about Blaze's mother? How does she feel about all of this? What is her involvement with her son?"

"I haven't gotten a real read from him, other than a few comments that suggested their relationship was respectful but limited. I gathered from other sources that she doesn't venture far from her husband's eye," Decker replied.

"I understand Blaze has two brothers?" Leah asked.

Decker nodded. "And an older sister, though Terry married her off to one of his client's sons the minute she was of legal age. Will probably do the same for the two brothers once they graduate from college and enter the family business, if you know what I mean."

Leah and I nodded. "Well, at least they were allowed to grow some facial hair and go to college," I murmured under my breath, before adding, "You get a sense of how the family feels about Anna?"

Decker looked like she'd belched up acid. "Blaze's father hit on her on at least one occasion, if that answers your question."

"I hadn't heard about that," I replied, forcing down my own bile baby.

Leah's reaction was to drop her pen and cover her ears. "Blaaah! How did Blaze react?"

"I'm not sure Blaze knows," Decker replied, not looking particularly comfortable about withholding that nugget from her client. "A friend of Anna's divulged the details on that one."

Leah released a growl and fisted her hands. "Anna probably figured that either AJ or I would have ratted the sicko out to the Stantons—we would have, in case you were interested—and they would have hunted the old perv down and hung him by the protruding parts of his anatomy."

"And she doesn't mean his nose," I offered.

Decker snorted before continuing, "It happened at a charity event. Anna was there on behalf of one of the Stanton's clients, taking one of her girlfriends as her plus one. At one point in the evening, the girlfriend went to the bar to grab drinks and when she returned, found Papa Edwards had pinned Anna in a corner. Before she could intervene, she overheard him tossing out a few suggestions about what he would like to do to her—while he forced Blaze to watch—so that he could 'show his son how a real man handled a woman'."

"Yuck," was all I could offer as Leah opened the window partway to spit, an uncharacteristic gesture that resulted in spittle down the side of Decker's vehicle.

Decker frowned. "Anyway, I'd pay good money for front row seats when the Stantons find out about it." She snorted before adding, "Heck, I'll throw in the rope."

"We'll bring the popcorn and adult beverages," Leah replied, wiping her mouth on the back of her hand.

"Better make mine a double," I said to no one in particular though I was graced with a round of head nods before Leah rolled the window all the way down and hocked another round of bile. "Make that a triple."

Rather than perpetuating a full-blown barf-o-rama of the

Stand by Me blueberry pie-eating contest variety, I elected to change the subject, directing my question at Decker.

"So, getting back to our suspect list—prior to the threats themselves—had Blaze encountered any other pushback?"

Decker paused to glance at Leah and nod at the window, probably hoping the spitting exercises had concluded. Leah scoffed but complied, rolling it up. Once satisfied, Decker returned to my question.

"Yeah. First, he got the runaround when he tried to procure the necessary permits. Then, there was an ecology group snooping around after they'd heard rumors Blaze was using the new project as a ruse so that he could film another extreme sports video. Whoever spewed that nonsense built it up with claims it was going to be the most outlandish creation to date, which would most definitely damage the beach."

"That's ridiculous. Any idea where the rumors started?" Leah asked.

I noticed she had yet to retrieve her pen. Rather than root around in the dark, she quickly extracted another from her seemingly bottomless tote bag of tricks. I was pretty sure it was the bag I had bought for her on her twenty-first birthday and didn't remember it being quite that massive.

Decker could only stare, somewhat amused, probably partially disgusted at the notion a woman needed a bag of that size.

"No," she responded, shaking her head, more at Leah than at the question she'd been asked. "I talked to a lot of them and actually found them to be pretty nice, respectful individuals who became concerned after receiving a rash of anonymous tips that referenced what Blaze was supposedly planning to do."

"Emails? Something traceable?" Leah asked, tapping her pen.

Decker shook her head. "Most of them were comments that came in on the group's social media feeds. Of course, shortly after the messages were sent, the accounts were deleted. The group insisted they were just doing their due diligence, checking Blaze out, making sure he was filming what he claimed he was. Once they went directly to the source, Blaze not only obliged their questions, he invited them to stick around during production. After a few days, most of them went away satisfied. A couple stayed on and even volunteered to be part of the crew. In the end, it was a win-win for both sides."

"That's a relief, except for the fact we've still got a whole lotta nothing when it comes to viable suspects and a grim reminder we've got limited time to catch up." Leah frowned as she relayed our current predicament, which was dismal, at best.

The three of us sat silently, staring out the window as we passed the "Welcome to Los Angeles" sign.

Part of me wanted to go back and bury my head in the sand of that luscious beach and pretend the previous hours were a cruel joke but deep inside I knew it would serve as nothing more than a temporary fix.

No, there was only one direction we could go and it wasn't the one in the view over my shoulder.

I blew out a long breath, catching Decker's eye in the rearview mirror. "You mentioned that you were working under-cover, that Bryce had come to the same conclusion as Anna had about the two of you." Decker nodded. "Do you think any of the other crew members had drawn the same conclusion? Or figured out the real reason you were there and felt Blaze had betrayed them—thinking he didn't trust them—or been flat out raging because they assumed you were spying on them?"

Perhaps "spying" was a harsh word but she had been there investigating them—or anything that led her to the culprit.

Before she could answer my phone rang.

"Anna," I murmured as I read the name on screen before answering.

"AJ!" My friend's voice was high-pitched as I placed her on

speakerphone so that we could all hear. "Where are you guys?"

"Just crossed into L.A., what's going on?" I replied, trying to keep my own voice calm.

"Blaze took off!" She shrieked into my ear. "Oh, Gawd, I don't know what I'm gonna do."

"Anna, I need you to calm down," I pleaded. "Where are you?"

"At Blaze's condo. I just got here and the living room is destroyed and there's blood everywhere—" Her breaths were rapid, as though she was panting.

"Anna, can you hear me?" I asked, noting the frowns from Leah and Decker. "Are you gonna pass out?"

"No." Her reply was weak.

"Just hang in there, we're on our way." I nodded at Decker, silently confirming she knew how to get to her. "In the meantime, take a couple of deep breaths—go outside if you need to for some fresh air." When I got no response, I added, "Anna, hon, can you do that for me?"

Another mumbled response was transmitted before we heard shuffling and then the passing of nearby cars.

"Okay, okay…I'm outside. I'm okay." I glanced at Leah who shook her head. Our friend was far beyond 'okay.'

"Whenever you're ready, tell us what happened," I replied.

After an extended pause, she huffed out a response. "I thought I was only a couple of minutes behind them, but they must have been really punching the gas because I was barely entering L.A. when I received a call from Blaze."

"What? I thought you and Blaze drove back together?" Leah asked.

"No, he wanted to talk to Cam privately and after the cops dropped them off at the beach, they hopped in Cam's truck—I guess one of the other crew was going to bring his bike from the accident site, so he didn't need to worry about going back.

Anyway, I lost sight of them but figured I'd get back to L.A. around the same time, shortly after Cam dropped Blaze at his place." Anna sniffled into the phone. "I was wrong. I should have insisted he come with me—maybe even that they both did—especially considering neither one of them was in any condition to drive."

"It is okay, Anna. You didn't do anything wrong…just tell us." I wanted to hug my friend, soothe whatever it was that had made her so upset. "What did Blaze say?"

"Oh Gawd, he was so frantic, so out-of-control. I could barely understand him but from what I could make out, on the way back, Blaze told Cam about everything—the investigation, Decker's real identity… and about Bryce."

Anna's voice was barely above a whisper. "Cam was furious. Understandably so. He blamed Blaze for Bryce's death…" She paused to catch her breath. "They argued and when Cam pulled up to Blaze's condo, Blaze stormed out…and Cam followed. Blaze said they got into a fight and by the looks of the condo, it must have been a pretty bad one."

"Is Blaze all right?" I asked. "What about Cam?"

"I don't know. I just don't know." Anna sounded out of breath, her words coming out in bursts and her voice ragged. "Blaze said he was knocked out for a few and when he woke up, Cam was gone."

"Where is Blaze now?" Leah asked.

"He was so incoherent…I can only assume he went after Cam," Anna replied, fully sobbing now. "All I know is that when I got there, both his car and Cam's truck were gone."

"What? He's driving? Could you tell how badly he was injured?" I tried to keep the fear out of my voice though I worried Blaze had suffered a concussion and was behind the wheel of a three-thousand-pound piece of metal.

"Blaze was definitely…not himself. I tried to keep him talking just to make sure he was okay, but he ended the call abruptly and now he's not answering. His calls just go straight to voicemail."

"What about Cam's place, would he go there?" Decker asked, indicating with her fingers that we were about five minutes away from reaching her.

"Yes, yes, especially if he was going after Cam!" Anna screeched into the phone. "Oh Gawd, I didn't mean it like that. It's just…given the condition of everything when I got here, I can only hope that when Blaze came to and saw all the blood and destruction he wanted to check on his friend. Or work things out."

Decker shook her head and frowned. I couldn't blame her. If the argument and subsequent fight were any indication of the current mindset of the two friends, making nice wouldn't have been on either one's immediate agenda. It was more likely that they intended to finish what they had started.

"We're a couple minutes out, Anna. Do you want us to swing by and grab you and then head toward Cam's?" Decker asked.

"Actually, I think it might be best if I stayed here, in case Blaze returns," Anna replied. "Would you mind shifting directions and heading straight there?" Without waiting for an answer, she started to relay the address but Decker cut her off.

"Already got it."

"Let me know," was the tired response from the other end of the connection. "No matter who…or what you find."

Once Anna disconnected, Decker turned to us. "I guess I should have asked if you were up for this."

"'Up for *this*'?" Leah glanced at me and snorted. "We were born for it."

Whether Decker was convinced, she was silent as she sharply turned the corner and sped toward our new destination, leaving us each to our thoughts.

Whatever it was we'd expected as we reached Cam's small house—none of us was fully prepared for what we found.

CHAPTER ELEVEN

Absolutely nothing.

And no one.

In fact, the dust that covered the packages on the front porch suggested Cam hadn't checked in at the old homestead for quite some time.

"Are you sure you've got the right address?" Leah asked, her tone as frustrated as it was accusatory.

Decker glared at her, then picked up one of the larger packages and shoved it in her face so that she could read the label. "You tell me."

Leah peered at it and nodded but offered no apology.

"Don't see his truck or Blaze's car anywhere on the street, either," Decker said as she scanned the street.

"Do you find this odd?" I asked her, thumbing at the vacant house and overflowing mailbox.

Decker shrugged. "Not really. Cam could be staying at his girlfriend's place."

"Yeah, I guess that's a possibility," I replied, dialing Anna's number as I surveyed Decker and wondered if she knew more than she was letting on.

I put a pin in that thought when Anna picked up on the first ring. Though she sounded a smidge calmer, the disappointment in her voice was unmistakable as she thanked me for the update when I shared our findings and let her know we'd make our way back to Blaze's once we were done.

After signing off, I noticed Decker snooping around the outside of Cam's house, peering in windows and over the gate leading to the backyard, which turned out to be locked.

"Anything?" I asked.

"Nothing more unusual than last time I was here," she replied, getting back into the SUV.

"When was that?" Leah asked as Decker drove in the direction we'd just come from, her pace no slower than it had previously been.

Decker was always on the job and apparently, always on a mission.

"Last week."

"So, you knew we wouldn't find anything." Leah frowned.

"Not so much knew as concluded." Decker shrugged. "A reasoned conclusion based upon his recent patterns."

"Then why…why waste the time?" Leah opened her hands.

"Wasn't a waste of time—it was a lead worth checking out. And we did," she replied.

I perused Decker's face. There was something about the set of her jaw convinced me she was being less than truthful.

"You wanted to make sure Anna wasn't with us when we went to check out Cam's, even though you knew he wouldn't be here." The twitch at the corner of Decker's mouth betrayed her. "Why?"

We'd traveled several miles before Decker offered me the courtesy of a response. "Because now we're going to stop by an alternate location—one that Cam is more likely to be at."

"The girlfriend's house?" I asked.

"No," When I cocked my head, she added, "A bar."

"After his throw down with Blaze, you think Cam decided to let off steam by tossing back a couple of shots?" The pitch of Leah's voice was as shrill as the notion was incredulous.

Decker shook her head. "The shots would be an added benefit. Nope, if he went to the bar, he went there to see his girlfriend."

"She works at the bar, I take?" Leah asked.

"She owns it," Decker replied.

"Then why does it matter whether Anna came along?" Leah tapping her fingers against the armrest.

I, too, wished Decker would get to the point.

"Because before she was Cam's girlfriend, she was also a… friend of Blaze's."

Apparently, the point had come sooner than expected, as Leah sat up rigidly in her seat and faced Decker, her eyes wide.

"You're not talking about *that* friend of Blaze's, are you?"

"You know then," Decker replied, smugly.

Leah did an amazing impression of a bobblehead. "I certainly do."

"Come on!" I growled from the backseat. "Would someone tell me what's going on? Or who?"

"You ever heard of Diamond Destiny?" Leah asked.

I scrunched my nose, trying to remember why the name sounded so familiar. "The chick who looks like Bo Derek's offspring, with the big coconuts and the multi-colored hair extensions? And, unless I'm mistaken, was in a handful of Blaze's films?"

Lead nodded. "That's the one."

If memory served, she got her nickname from wearing itsy bitsy diamond-encrusted bikinis whenever performing her stunts which, to the delight of many sports enthusiasts, displayed a level of buoyancy that defied the laws of gravity. She was like the whipped cream on top of the hot fudge sundae...not necessary but definitely an added bonus one would be a fool to turn down.

"Huh. So she's friends with Blaze…big deal." I shrugged.

Leah shook her head. "Not *that* kind of friend, AJ. Before Blaze and Anna got together, it was rumored the two of them were…very close."

"Not a rumor," Decker added. "Several of the crew say she still blames Anna for their breakup."

My mouth formed an "o" as I formulated a response. "Does Anna know…about the animosity, I mean?"

Decker nodded. "She does, but she only became aware of it after-the-fact." After taking in our confused expressions, she added, "Blaze said there had been an…incident between the two women early on in Blaze and Anna's relationship. Anna showed up to one of Blaze's shoots, which Destiny was in, and things got…ugly. To this day, Blaze insists they were finished before he and Anna got together."

"What do you think?" I asked, sensing her doubt.

"I tend to defer to there being three sides to any situation," she replied.

"Only with Cam being part of the mix now, there are four," Leah added.

"Probably more," was Decker's response.

We rode in silence until Decker parked across the street from an establishment aptly named after its owner. From the outside, it appeared to be a tribute to the beach bum and surfer types. I could only imagine what was beyond the doors, which were crafted out of surfboards.

Decker noted that Cam's truck—an old white Toyota Land Cruiser with a massive ski rack mounted on the roof—was not present. The other vehicle Decker had described she was on the lookout for—a 1969 Pontiac GTO in midnight blue and a pretty distinctive ride at that—was parked in the bar's parking lot.

After getting out and checking the plates, she confirmed it belonged to the other person we sought.

Blaze.

CHAPTER TWELVE

"Somebody's got some 'splaining to do," Leah murmured.

"You know, a case could be made he came here looking for Cam." I slid a glance at her and of course, she knew I was serving up a sarcasm sandwich.

Decker watched our exchange, shaking her head as she opened the door to the bar. The smell of sweat, booze and an odor that eerily smelled like a skunk wafted out, forcing me to fight the urge to gag as we entered.

Leah scrunched her nose. "Is that…"

"Weed," Decker said, low enough so that only the two of us could hear. "For medicinal purposes, of course."

"Whatever ails ya, I guess," Leah replied, scowling as she pinched her nose between her thumb and forefinger.

Even though the bar was nearly three-quarters full with people dancing to the jukebox, playing pool, shooting darts or just hanging out in small groups, we quickly found Blaze standing at the bar, waving his hands as he talked to the woman on the other side.

He'd been easy to spot, not because we knew what he looked

like but because his loud, angry voice made him hard to ignore as several patrons moved away. Blood had formed clumps in his usually perfectly tousled hair and coagulated on his split lip. His clothes were ripped to the point one sleeve clung by only a few threads, his feet were barefoot and filthy and his hands and knuckles were covered in makeshift bandages, many of which had bleed through. One particularly bad gash on his palm was exposed, leaving stains on his pint glass as a macabre aftereffect.

The woman behind the bar frowned at something he was saying and thrust a forefinger into his chest as she leaned within millimeters of his face and responded through gritted teeth. Blaze shook his head and threw up his hands as she spun on her heel and stalked away.

Now that I'd seen her in the flesh—I realized I had underestimated Diamond Destiny. Even behind those Bo Derek looks and wildly-colored locks, the only thing reminiscent of her teeny weeny bikini days was the ample showing of bosom, prominently displayed by the low-cut t-shirt sporting the bar's name. Grimacing as I noted the pair of guns she had working, I was betting she could have given Decker a run for her money. Having said that, Blaze—whether he realized it or not—had gotten off lucky. This time.

"Blaze," Decker called out as we approached.

He picked up his pint glass and chugged its contents within a few gulps before slamming it on the bar.

"What the hell are you doing here?" He asked without even a glance in her direction, fisting both hands on the bar.

Decker sidled up to the seat next to his and faced him.

"Looking for Cam. And yet, found you."

Blaze snorted and from his slurred speech, it was clear he was either a light-weight or had already pounded several beverages.

"Well, as your beady little eyes can see, that rat-bastard is not here." He cartoonishly gestured around the bar with one arm before pausing. "Wait—how did you know?" He tapped his head. "Ahh, sweet Anna. Where is my raven-haired goddess? And why hasn't she come to fetch me?"

Or save him from himself, I thought to myself, shocked by what I was witnessing. One would be hard-pressed to deny it had been a long, hard day but I had never seen him in such a mood. It was not a look he wore well. It was probably for the best that Anna wasn't around to see him in this manner. She had enough on her plate, taking in nearly as much, if not more than Blaze had in the short time since we had landed in town.

Apparently, Decker was no more amused than the rest of us as she stared him down, her tone sour as she responded, "At your condo. Waiting for you." Blaze broke away from her piercing gaze and Decker added, "You do remember calling her." It settled in as more of a jab than a question.

Blaze ignored it, tipping his empty glass on its side and spinning it. "Where's Cam, then, Ms. P.I.?"

"That's what we should be asking you," Decker replied, her eyes never leaving him. "What exactly did you do to your friend? And where the hell is he?"

"I have no idea." Blaze hung his head, frowning. "She didn't know, either."

He gestured down the bar toward Destiny, who was busy pouring fresh beers for a couple at the other end. When she caught him staring she glared and turned her back, causing him to huff.

"Said he hasn't been here and that he's not responded to any of her calls. Mine either."

"Just what did you expect, Blaze?"

"Don't start with me, Decker," he spat out as he shot her an angry look. "You...you started this."

I gave her a heck of a lot of credit—Decker stood her ground. "No Blaze. Let's be straight. Whoever's been threatening you and your crew started this. You brought me in to end it."

Blaze returned his glass to an upright position and slammed it onto the bar top with such force he caught a variety of looks from patrons—not to mention a venomous one from Destiny.

"Yeah, well, you've done a stellar job to this point, Decker."

"Not interested in your sarcasm, Blaze. Perhaps you should take it easy on the grown-up beverages," she replied, reaching for his glass.

Blaze clumsily snatched it away and attempted to stare her down, though his eyes were barely slits and weren't focusing on anything in particular.

Finally, he snorted and managed to slur out, "You tell your pops that, did ya, Decker? Maybe if he hadn't been hitting the bottle so hard, he would have caught your poor mama's killer before he met his maker."

I sucked in a breath as he tossed back his head and released a repulsive howl, slapping the man to his left on the back as he did. The man had the good graces to look away and move to another seat.

In hindsight, it would be the first, and only, time I would see Decker break out of character—a flash of anger sparked in her eyes as she ground her jaw, balling her hands into fists. In that moment, I witnessed the rage and saw what was within the core of her being and perhaps—at some level—her soul.

It was both frightening…and familiar.

And then, just like that, it was gone.

I'm not sure what happened but somehow, somewhere she dug down deep inside and suddenly, the emotion evaporated and the anger turned to nothing more than a squint as she leaned in so close Blaze must have felt the heat of her breath on his ear.

"Let's not forget, I told you to tell them…all of them…about me…about everything…for weeks…and yet, you refused."

Blaze tempted fate, continuing his belligerent antagonism. "And we know how well that sage advice turned out, don't we?"

Decker slapped him up the backside of the head but he was so far gone, he was starting to look like a bobblehead. Even when he released a slow hiss, she would not be swayed. Her smile turned cruel, almost demonic as she replied and though her tone was sharp there was no humor behind it.

"Get real, Blaze. You aren't seriously arrogant—or ignorant— enough to place the blame for what happened to Bryce…*on me*?"

"No, Decker. I blame myself. For hiring you," he replied through gritted teeth. "And I blame Abe and Elijah for recommending you and to be honest, I seriously don't even want to be looking at your face right now, much less wasting any more of what time I have left on this earth talking to you."

"Touché. Consider our business concluded. I'll send you a bill tomorrow. Now that we know where you are, we'll be on our way." Decker's unnerving smile remained intact as she added, "As a parting piece of advice—on the house—call your fiancé and let her know that while you are a complete jackass, you're still alive. Better yet, call a cab and go show her."

"Go to hell, Decker. Like you give a rat's—"

Before he could finish that original comeback, Decker moved past him and strode toward Destiny, who had been intently watching the entire exchange.

I patted Blaze on the shoulder and Leah leaned into him, whispering as we followed Decker, "Please, do call her, Blaze. She's a wreck. One of us can drive you back."

Blaze nodded, though it was clear he wasn't absorbing her message as he glared at Decker, who was engaged in a discussion with his former peer and girlfriend.

"At least I tried," Leah mumbled to my back as we moved through the crowd to join the two unlikely cohorts.

"Probably better than he deserved," I replied over my shoulder. "But we owe it to Anna. How she chooses to deal with it is up to her."

We sidled up to Decker, who promptly introduced us to Destiny, who in turn offered us both a firm handshake and a warm smile. As she perused us, I realized Diamond Destiny was definitely more than met the eye. Once you got past her exterior, there was a spark behind those icy blue eyes, which were filled with excitement and an intelligence that suggested she was wise to ways of the world. I doubted she minded that people underestimated her and was sure she used it to her advantage.

"Decker's been filling me in on everything that Blaze was too incoherent to spit out. Just a shame to hear about Bryce." Destiny shook her head. "Another righteous dude gone far too soon and though I never believed he'd leave this life the easy way, I always thought it would be on his terms. Guess the universe had other plans. It's always a somber reminder that while we think we've got the world in the palm of our hands, we're never really in control. Of anything."

There was a moment of silence before she added, "And now, this fight between Cam and Blaze? That one I definitely didn't see coming. I'm glad you showed up when you did. Not that it excuses his behavior but at least it explains it."

Decker nodded. "You mentioned calling him a cab?"

"Yeah, it's shown up and gone. Flat out refused it, threatened to sit outside all night and wait for Cam to show." Destiny turned to us. "I was just telling Decker that I haven't heard from him since this morning. Not by phone or in the flesh."

"Could he have stopped by your place? Gone there to clean up, take a shower, that kind of thing?" Leah asked.

"This *is* my place." Destiny went on to explain that she had a small apartment at the back of the bar.

"Convenient," Leah murmured.

Destiny nodded. "We're open seven days a week and considering the bar is in my name, I like to be hands on. Not to mention, it's pretty much my livelihood these days, though there is still the homage to my previous life." She waved a hand at the décor before adding, "I'm sure Decker has supplied all the gory details on that topic." She laughed after catching our guilty expressions. "I simply meant my stint in—and retirement from—extreme sports."

"By choice," Decker added.

"Oh yeah, always." Destiny laughed. "Not that I consider age a factor but I'd lost my appetite for it. It was getting harder and harder to drum up fresh material—stuff that our diehard fans wouldn't already anticipate. I think a lot of us never realized we should have gotten out before we did and by then, it was either too late or we ended up dead.

"I didn't want that for myself and while this bar may look like a dive, it's mine—something that's physical and tangible—and it provides something for the community, even if it's just a drink after a hard day, or a group of friends to commiserate with…or like Blaze, somewhere to go when you're lost or have got nowhere else to go."

"Well, judging from all the photographs lining the walls, you've got something good going here. There are some pretty famous faces up there," Leah replied, pointing at a picture of a current A-list actor.

Destiny shrugged. "Guess it depends on how you define fame. You know what I mean, Decker." She nodded at photo of an older man that looked oddly like Decker, except for as the fact he was clearly intoxicated and in a precarious situation with a pair of double Ds.

Decker barely glanced at the photo, her expression unchanged as Destiny continued, "For example, that skinny dude over by the pool table? He's a single father of three. Works as an EMT—arguably one of the toughest jobs out there. Brought two children—babies really—back from the dead just this afternoon, after their babysitter left them in a hot car while she went into the mall to see her boyfriend.

"Or that chick at the table to the right of him—the one with the obnoxious shade of red hair? She was able to convince a battered wife to leave her abusive husband and get herself and her children into a safe refuge before he made good on his threat to kill her next time he saw her.

"*They* are the ones that truly deserve the fame." She shook her head and frowned before adding, "They make a difference in this world and expect nothing in return, while some of us demand it purely to soothe our over-inflated egos."

"We all serve a purpose, Destiny," Decker replied firmly, her tone sincere. "We just have to find our passion and know that when we put ourselves out in the world, both it and everyone in it are getting the very best versions of us. Because we love what we do."

Destiny reached a fist across the bar and knocked it against Decker's. "Anyone ever tell you that you're a hell of lot wiser than you let on?"

Decker hacked out a laugh. "Just my pops. And that was only when I bested him at his own game." When she caught our confused expressions, she added, "I solved a case he couldn't crack."

Destiny started to reply but got derailed as she glanced down to the bar, frowning.

"We've got ourselves a little problem, gals."

We followed her line of sight and released a collective groan.

The spot Blaze had previously occupied was empty.

"Well, crap," Decker growled as we proceeded to the front of the bar and out into the brisk air.

On the ground, a pint glass had been smashed across the asphalt.

And that gorgeous 1969 Pontiac GTO in midnight blue?

Gone.

CHAPTER THIRTEEN

After the initial shock wore off—and several expletives were tossed out into the stratosphere—we alerted Anna, hoping Blaze would return to the condo in one piece, though holding no illusions he would even return to his home.

Cam, after all, was not there and Blaze would not stop searching for him until his mission was complete.

Unfortunately, the alcohol he'd ingested would not only serve as a danger to himself but everyone on the road he came into contact with. But as terrifying as that prospect was, I was far more concerned with the outcome of a reunion between Blaze and his friend. If round two came to fruition, I wouldn't want to bear witness to the aftermath.

It was no surprise that Anna was less than thrilled to learn where we'd located him and even more frustrated that he'd escaped in an impaired condition. Out of respect, we were silent until she finished her rant, at which point, she noted our silence and quickly added that she wasn't angry at us, specifically, for failing to prevent what she described as an inevitable situation, after what the duo had been through that day.

She did express confusion and said that she could count on

one hand the number of times Blaze had overindulged in alcohol. And, more importantly, she couldn't recall any situation where he'd actually been ignorant enough to think he could get into a vehicle and drive. She sighed as she mentioned having a few friends on the police force she could call to keep an eye out for Blaze's car.

Of course, she also realized that if Blaze was spotted, law enforcement would be bound to intervene, which would result in an arrest and jail time. The laws were strict and even Blaze's father would not be able to get him out of trouble this time.

"Wouldn't be the worst thing," Decker responded when Anna finished. "At least we'd know where one of them was."

"I just hope Cam's fate doesn't end up the same or worse. I can also have them look for his truck and hopefully by the end of this hellacious day, we'll have them both back where they belong," Anna replied.

And both in one piece, I thought to myself.

We agreed to head back to Blaze's, where Decker would drop us and we'd help Anna clean up the mess in his condo. Decker indicated she wanted to check on a few things and would meet up with us in the morning.

We said our goodbyes to Destiny and made an agreement to keep one another up to date. She kept her concern for Cam close to the vest, assuring us he was just probably too embarrassed to have shown his face in the bar until she'd closed for the night. That was several hours away and personally, I wouldn't have been able to keep the worst of thoughts from emerging, much less sit still, while waiting for him to return.

No, if I had been Destiny, I would have left my bartender in charge, jumped in my car and scoured the city and all of his known haunts, dialing his number nonstop, until I could sock him in the gut for making me worry. After we left, I said as much to Leah, which of course, Decker overheard.

"Don't blame her for not reacting with more emotion. She's known Blaze, Bryce, Cam—all of them—for a long time. And, she's definitely been through worse."

"Worse than death?" Leah snorted, before adding, "Because honestly, I can't conjure anything worse than that, no matter how resilient—or bull-headed—you all are. Dead is dead and unlike the supernatural zombie crap, resurrection in this realm is purely fiction." With that, she spun on her heel, stomped to Decker's vehicle and jumped in the back alongside Nicoh, who'd slept through the entire outing.

"Don't take it personally," I said to Decker, who stared at Leah sitting rigidly in her SUV. "This hits a little too close to home for her—for both of us. Death has come knocking at our doorstep one too many times. After a while, even though the wound is no longer bleeding it never seems to completely heal."

"Tell me about it," she murmured, hopping into the driver's seat while I rode shotgun this time around. "I've been picking at that scab all my damn life."

We rode in silence, except for Nicoh, who chewed on his paw. It was a welcome break from the accident site and the subsequent scene at the bar. I opened the window and allowed the evening air to whip strands of my hair into a frenzied mess.

Before long, Decker dropped us at Blaze's condo and as we entered, we found Anna on her knees, scraping the remnants of a table lamp into a dustpan.

Without as much as a glance or a hello, she pointed at an over-turned entertainment center, its contents scattered in various conditions throughout the room.

"Not much assistance when it comes electronics repair," Leah grumbled, picking up what was left of the blu-ray player.

"Idiots," Anna mumbled, dumping the dustpan into the garbage can, before picking up a trophy in the shape of a surfboard. She wiped it clean with a rag before placing it back on the shelf and moving onto the next.

Though she hadn't said much since our arrival, it was hard not to notice that her words were slurred. And while she hadn't been drinking, she also hadn't eaten the entire time we'd been in L.A.

Gosh, had it only been a day? I thought wearily.

Leah, Nicoh and I hadn't eaten either, but we'd had more than enough snacks on the trip prior that would have allowed a small village to survive for a week. Anna, on the other hand, was not only skin and bones, she was exhausted, both physically and emotionally. I feared she would collapse at any moment. Leah noticed the same and quickly grabbed her phone.

"Anna, name your fave takeout spot in this area."

"New Garden has amazing chop suey. Wait—they aren't open this late during the week."

"Uh, sorry to be the bearer of bad news but think you might have lost a day…it's Saturday," Leah replied.

Anna frowned. "Oh, gosh, you are absolutely right. I'll take that chop suey then, with brown rice," she replied before reciting the phone number from memory.

I nodded at Leah, who offered a smile in return. The fact that Anna entertained the idea of food was a positive sign. Once the order was placed, we resumed the cleanup session while we waited for it to be delivered.

"Did you get any more information? Or hear from anyone?" I asked as I sorted through the CDs I'd collected, noting only a few had been irrevocably damaged.

Anna shook her head. "Called everyone I could think of and no one has seen or heard from him."

"Would any of them cover for him, if he insisted he wanted to be alone?" Leah asked.

Anna rehung a few pictures, pausing for a moment. "I don't think so but honestly, I don't know."

"What about his family?" I asked.

"Absolutely *not*—I know that for a fact. It wouldn't have even been a consideration. His father would pitch a fit if he showed up at his parent's estate in that condition, given what you described of Blaze's behavior at the bar."

Leah nodded. "Speaking of his father, we heard about your recent…encounter with him."

Anna looked at each of us, her eyes wide. After a moment, she shook her head. "I should have known Decker would dig up all the juicy details."

"Does Blaze know?" I asked.

"Yeah, it's yet another reason I know that he'd never go to his family."

"We know his relationship with his father is challenged, but what about his mother?" Leah suggested.

"Not a chance. She's barely more than Terrence's sock puppet. Does as he does. Mimics his thoughts, feelings, behaviors. Probably the only thing that she has that's her own is a healthy inheritance. Her family was into vineyards."

"Was?" I asked.

"Her father sold them for a small fortune back in the 1950s. Blaze's mother, Celeste, was the only living heir and had expressed zero interest in taking over the family business, so he decided to sell it off before he passed so she couldn't run it into the ground. Let's just say, Celeste is not a very business-minded person. In fact, she's led a very sheltered life, first with her parents and then with Terrence, and prefers being taken care of and being on the arm of a very rich man. I'm sure this pleases Terrence to no end, as she's definitely more pliable that way."

"She's likely oblivious to his philandering," Leah mused. "Or doesn't care."

"Exactly. The man—father-in-law-to-be or not—is a pig," Anna replied through gritted teeth.

That bile-producing conversation ended when the doorbell rang and we eagerly scarfed up every last bite of our food. Not even a crab puff was spared, to Nicoh's despair, as he was relegated to his normal portion of kibble. I won't go into nauseating detail about it, but he had a lot to say about it before slinking off into a corner of Bryce's condo and gracing us with his backside.

When the humans finished their meal, Anna fished in her bag, pulled out a set of keys and tried to hand them to me. "Here, why don't you take my vehicle, go back to my condo and get some rest."

I shook my head and Leah did the same. "We're not leaving you here alone. Once Blaze shows up, we'll take your suggestion under consideration. And before you protest, keep in mind that while you may be able to kick our butts with that fancy black belt, you're not gonna force him to budge."

I pointed at Nicoh, who snored softly, his form partially wedged under the coffee table, where he'd snuck in closer at some point, hoping to capture a loose morsel or two. When none presented itself, he'd rewarded himself with another nap.

"How can he sleep at a time like this?" Anna released a small chuckle.

"He's had a hard day." I smirked. "Then again, based on his soulful howls when the food arrived—they're *all* hard days."

Anna's smile fell away. "Tell me about it."

* * *

Morning came and Blaze never showed or called. I'd heard Anna fidgeting and pacing throughout the night in Blaze's room. I couldn't say that I got much sleep either, despite the cushiness of the couch. Even Leah was sporting a couple of nasty bags under her eyes as she stumbled out of the guest bedroom, plucking at flattened clumps of hair.

The only one not in a foul mood turned out to be the canine, who amused himself by chasing his tail while the humans tapped our fingers on the countertop as we waited for the coffeemaker to finish its brew.

After we'd downed the entire pot, we locked Blaze's freshly-straightened condo and started piling into Anna's vehicle.

And that's when things got weird.

Nicoh uncharacteristically growled and gnashed his teeth when I opened the rear passenger door and urged him to jump in, as he pulled on his lead and twisted his head in an attempt to break free. My commands were ignored as he tugged and thrashed, half-barking, half-howling.

"Whoa!" Anna exclaimed when he caught me off-guard and I stumbled backward.

"Nicoh!" I shouted, securing my footing and facing him head on. "What the heck?"

His eyes were like saucers as he continued to tug, his howls intensifying as he struggled to back away from the vehicle.

Leah frowned, shaking her head as she put in her earbuds and cranked up the tunes to block him out.

Anna glanced at me, wide-eyed but I nodded that I had things under control so she inserted the key into the ignition, turned it and slapped her hand against the steering wheel when the engine failed to turn over, resulting in nothing more than a pathetic click, click, click.

"You've got to be kidding me," she grumbled. "All of this *and* a dead battery, too?"

Nicoh continued to bark and howl, even more high-pitched and frenzied. I wondered if someone had hijacked my dog or injected some sort of wacky serum into him. Just as Anna started to turn the key I reflected on her last words, "all of this and a dead battery, too…" and Bryce's angry face flashed in my head as he stormed away from us at the beach.

"Stop, Anna, no!" I screamed, releasing Nicoh's lead so that I could swat her arm. She started to pull the key out and I screamed, "No!"

Leah pulled her earbuds out. "What?" She looked from me to Nicoh to Anna, wondering if we'd all gone loco.

"Get out! There's something wrong!" I yelled and finally, something connected as she grabbed her bag, opened the door and made a break for it.

Leah, Nicoh and I followed suit and we didn't stop until we were several hundred feet away, huddled behind a brick wall, fully convinced we were about to find ourselves in the middle of an apocalypse, set in motion when Anna's SUV turned into a loaded weapon. But nothing came.

Still, we waited.

And nothing came.

All of us jumped—Leah might have screamed—when my phone rang.

I didn't recognize the number but for whatever reason, decided to answer it.

"Hello?" I whispered.

"AJ?" It was a familiar voice, one that I hadn't expected.

"Abe?"

Leah and Anna exchanged worried glances at the mention of the elder Stanton brother's name.

"You sound out of breath. Did I catch you in the middle of something? I thought you'd be with Anna but she wasn't answering, so I called you, knowing you'd be in town by now."

"Uh, kinda…working through something…Anna's here, though," I replied as she shook her head from side to side—in no way was she prepared to deal with him.

Leah had other ideas, calling out, "Hey Stanton, you may wanna give one of your buds on the bomb squad a quick buzz… we might have a live one here."

"Is that Campbell?" Abe replied, sounding mildly amused.

I gritted my teeth at Leah and made a slashing gesture across my throat.

"It is," I replied, hoping he hadn't heard her entire request.

"What's that about a bomb squad?" He asked, causing me to stifle a groan.

I could only imagine Abe on the other end, preparing to jump into his Ferrari, probably with Elijah riding shotgun, recklessly endangering other motorists, pedestrians and animal—vermin or otherwise—as they raced back from Las Vegas to L.A. to handle matters themselves.

Leah winced when I shook my head, as Anna frowned and extended her hand, taking the phone.

"Got Frank's number handy?" she asked, holding the phone away from her ear as a barrage of expletives erupted from the other end of the connection.

Once the Stanton brother took a breath, Anna gritted her teeth as she reiterated her request, "Just the number...please." More commentary ensued before the information was relayed, to which she responded, "Thanks, will call you later."

Anna disconnected before he could protest, dialing the number he had supplied. After a brief explanation to Frank, she handed my phone back.

"He'll be here within fifteen." Anna rustled around in her bag and then checked her pockets. Her eyes widened. "Oh, crap."

"What?" Both Leah and I said in tandem.

"My phone's in there." She nodded toward the vehicle.

"Whoops." I winced, before adding, "This Frank dude, he can handle...problems of this nature?" Anna offered a single head nod. "Is he in law enforcement?"

"Ex-military but yeah, he's pretty good tackling stuff like this —whatever it is we're dealing with."

"You're hoping to keep this on the down-low," Leah commented.

Anna nodded. "I'd prefer not to get law enforcement involved, if at all possible. Am hoping maybe this gaff will allow us to get a leg up on the jerk behind the threats. The longer he believes he's gotten away with it or is not aware he hasn't made good on this particular threat—" She paused, shuddering. "Let's just say, we've gotta take any advantage we're given."

Though my body parts hadn't been scattered throughout the neighborhood, I still wasn't sure I consider it an advantage and said as much.

"You do realize he was here, outside, watching us last night."

"That's an uncomfortable thought," Leah replied, frowning.

Anna didn't respond as she looked from Blaze's building to the vehicle. I did the same and then perused the street for an ideal hiding place.

I pointed at an overgrown cropping of bushes in the complex adjacent to Blaze's. "That looks suspect."

Anna squinted, looking back toward the condo as she gauged the distance. "Let's check it out."

The four of us jogged over and started searching the area. If anyone just happened to glance out of their windows, there were going to be flashing lights and handcuffs in our futures. Nicoh sniffed, while Leah and I searched the ground, getting on our hands and knees when something looked interesting, Anna walked the perimeter and checked for vantage points for both Anna's vehicle and the condo.

"Anything?" she asked after a few more minutes, plucking a few stray leaves from her hair.

"Nope," I replied, brushing dirt and debris from my jeans.

Even Nicoh had collected it in his fur and had some tangled in his tail.

"I still think this is the place." Anna frowned as she scanned the area one final time. "Good line of sight of both my SUV and Blaze's condo."

"Yeah, well it appears as though his peeping skills are superior to his skills as a saboteur," Leah grumbled.

I winced and shook my head at Leah, who clamped a hand over her mouth.

"I think I'll let Frank be the judge of that," Anna replied, kicking a dirt clod so hard it exploded onto the street, spraying particles of dust in every direction. "But from where we're standing right now, it seems to me his successes have far outweighed his failures."

Leah started to speak as a blue minivan pulled up and a stout middle-aged man with cropped hair that was graying at the temples hustled toward us, his t-shirt and jeans stained in undecipherable shades of green, pink and orange.

"Gotta make this quick. Margie's pulling a double in the ER and is coming off shift at zero eleven hundred. I called the sitter in, but the gal has to be in class at zero ten thirty. Gonna have to pay her extra as it is, 'cause Mattie's got the croup and Dylan's teething… And if Margie catches wind I left 'em alone, my butt's out in the backyard with the dogs for the next week and a half." He barely paused to breathe. "So, get to it woman, what are we working with here?" He nodded at Anna's SUV.

I glanced at Leah, who could only stare at the man, her mouth open as her lip quivered. I'd seen the look before. On Nicoh. She was, in a word, dumbfounded.

Anna quickly made introductions then filled him in on everything—including Nicoh's reaction—before we'd opted to skedaddle and huddle behind the block wall.

When she finished, Frank glanced at Nicoh, nodding in a way that suggested he was impressed. "Is he trained?"

I shrugged. "Not for something like this. And, honestly, even the stuff he has been trained to do is based on his mood or whether it's nearing his dinner time."

Further proving my point, Nicoh chose that moment to entertain himself by chasing his tail, which was hinged under his back leg, causing him to fall mid-spin.

Frank frowned—possibly retracting his first impression—before turning his attention toward the SUV.

"Stay put while I check this out."

There was no argument from the three of us. Nicoh didn't count because he was too busy attacking the foot on the leg that had forced him to the ground. I sighed as Leah shook her head and rolled her eyes, already familiar with Nicoh's shtick.

After several minutes, Frank returned, handing Anna her cell phone as he tilted his head in Nicoh's direction while holding up a contraption that looked like a mangled mass of wires and gadgets.

"This guy probably saved your life."

Anna's eyes widened. "Is that what I think it is?" Frank nodded. "Did you get it all?"

This time, Frank just stared.

"Err, sorry." She bit her lip before adding, "You'll keep this quiet like we agreed?"

"Unless something arises and I'm asked in an official capacity," he replied.

Anna nodded. "Thanks. How much do I owe you?"

Frank waved a hand and turned to leave, stopping to scratch Nicoh under the chin. "Just tell Abe to deduct it from my tab."

We watched as he strode back to the minivan. It wasn't until he pulled away and out of sight that Leah looked at Anna.

"*Deduct* it from his tab? Wouldn't you think it would be the other way around?"

"I have no idea," Anna replied. "And I'm not sure I want to."

We gingerly got back into Anna's SUV. It took some persuading on Nicoh's part—along with a handful of doggie treats and a new rawhide bone—but we finally got everyone tucked in and were heading back to Anna's condo to get cleaned up when Decker called.

Anna placed her on speakerphone and quickly filled her in on our unwelcomed surprise. When she finished, we heard Decker release a long breath.

"Crap. I really hate to pile on top but I have an update and I wanted to contact you before you found out from someone else."

We looked at one another and released a collective groan, to which Anna added, "Might as well bring it on. This day has already started on a fabulous note, so it's not like things could get much worse."

"Kinda wish you hadn't said that," Decker replied. "It's about Blaze."

"You found him?" Anna asked.

"I didn't find him," Decker replied. "The police did. He's in jail."

Anna smacked the steering wheel with the palm of her hand.

"Gah—that idiot got himself busted for a DUI—I am going to kick his butt all the way across the ocean for being so stupid!"

Decker sighed. "Unfortunately, it's worse than that."

"Come on, Decker. What could be worse than a DUI?" Anna snapped.

I could think of something and hoped Decker wouldn't say it.

Like luck, hope only gets you so far.

"Murder."

CHAPTER FOURTEEN

"Have you lost your freaking mind, Decker?" Anna yelled at the phone.

"I'm just a messenger here, Goodwin. Let's not get nasty." Decker's voice was sharp.

Anna huffed out a breath. "It's just been a rough day."

"Unfortunately, it's about to get a lot worse."

Decker clearly wasn't one for doling out sympathy.

Anna scoffed as she maneuvered her massive vehicle through rush hour traffic. "Well, they can't charge him with murder when they haven't found a body—"

Decker interjected, "Actually, surfers found a body in a cove a couple of miles over from where Blaze's crew has been filming. It hadn't been there long—"

"Oh, God. They found Bryce." Anna fought to keep the vehicle in the lane as tears threatened the corner of her eyes.

"Not Bryce," Decker replied. "He's still out there…somewhere."

"I don't understand. If not Bryce, then who are we talking about?" Anna's voice was so shrill, Leah reached over to grasp her free hand in an attempt to calm her, casting me a wide-eyed glance as she did.

"It was Cam, Anna." Decker sounded tired, almost resigned. "It was Cam."

Anna pulled the vehicle over and we sat in silence for a moment. It was a lot to absorb within such a short amount of time. I touched Anna's arm but she continued to stare out the window, so I left her to her silence.

"He drowned?" Leah's voice came out sounding like the squeaky toy Nicoh had destroyed two minutes after I'd bought it.

"Nope. Pretty sure he didn't drown," Decker replied.

"How do you know?" Anna finally spoke, her voice quiet as she squinted at the traffic surrounding us.

"I know because I was there," Decker replied. Before we could ask, she added, "Shortly after the surfers found him, one of them called me. I had handed out enough cards over the last few months and had made the rounds to nearly every beach, asking them to let me know if anything odd occurred or seemed out of whack, no matter how small. The dude not only managed to remember our conversation, he'd kept my card in his Jeep and gave me a call. Just dumb luck, I guess."

"Did the surfers know who he was after they pulled him out?" I asked.

"Nope, just that I was interested in receiving a call if anything out of the ordinary occurred. This definitely fit the bill," Decker replied.

Had the killer managed to get his hands on one of those cards? I wondered. Something else was nagging me. "How did *you* get there so fast?"

Decker never missed a beat. "I was at the beach, looking for Blaze. Found him wandering around…acting like a fool. Nothing good was going to come of that, so I took him with me and that's when all hell broke loose."

"Another altercation?" Leah asked.

"No, I thought he'd be better off staying in the vehicle where he could sleep it off. Unfortunately, someone spotted him and told the officers that he'd seen a guy resembling Blaze at the beach earlier, fighting with another dude. He claimed the other dude stumbled and fell after being hit and didn't get back up. After checking on him, he said Blaze ran. The witness followed him for a bit but couldn't keep up and eventually lost sight of him—until he saw him sitting in my vehicle. Said he recognized Blaze from his clothing."

"Convenient, this guy just happening to peek through your window," I replied. "Who was he, anyway?"

"From what I gathered, just some homeless guy who sleeps in the same section of beach each night and notices everything that goes on."

"Hmm, sounds completely credible." Leah snorted. "Did you get a chance to talk to him?"

"No, in the hubbub, he managed to slip away, which is just too coincidental for my liking."

"You've got to be kidding." Anna sighed, shaking her head. "And still, they insisted on hauling Blaze in, based on the word of this so-called witness?"

"Unfortunately, Blaze was in no condition to be of any assistance—at least not until he'd dried up—and they couldn't just afford to let him go," Decker replied, her voice stern as she added, "I certainly wasn't about to risk my reputation on Blaze after the behavior we witnessed yesterday."

"Don't tell me you believe this homeless guy's story?" Anna frowned.

"I don't want to believe it but Blaze did get into it with Cam just hours prior and then went on to make a complete ass of himself at Destiny's. I don't know, maybe they met up and continued where they left off," Decker replied. "Regardless, the cops felt the story was compelling enough to hold him."

"Fabulous." Anna tugged at her ponytail, pulling the band free and tossing it onto the dashboard. "So what else did this witness have to say?"

"Nothing. Like I said, other than the description of Blaze, he slipped into the crowd of looky-loos and disappeared before I could have a go at him," Decker rumbled into the phone.

"What if the witness' account was all a setup, contrived by our perp?" I asked. "He could have handed the homeless guy a twenty and told him to bail."

"Or killed him after he'd completed his task," Leah added. "After all, who would miss a homeless person?"

"Interesting thought, but the perp would have to have known about the first fight," Decker replied.

Anna sat up. "That wouldn't have been too hard. We already know he was spying on us at Blaze's. He could have simply taken advantage of an opportunity, once it was presented to him."

I nodded. "He could have been at the bar, too."

"AJ's right. He could've been anybody and we wouldn't have known," Leah replied, nibbling on a nail before adding, "Chances are he knows everything we know and if that's the case, then he's gotta be feeling pretty confident."

Both women frowned at me. I noticed that Decker had been particularly quiet for some time.

"What do you think, Decker?" My question was met with awkward silence, so I tried again. "Uh, Decker, you're being awfully quiet."

"Sorry I dropped out. I had to put you on mute for a few." Her breathing was labored, as though she was walking fast or had been running.

"Where are you, anyway?" I realized we'd never asked.

"I'm still here," she replied, before adding clarification, "at the beach."

"And?" The three of us said in concession.

"I just caught a glimpse of the body," Decker replied, panting. "Cam took a significant beating. And while

I'm no M.E, I pretty sure Blaze's fist didn't produce the crater-sized hole in the back of his skull."

CHAPTER FIFTEEN

Whether she paused again to catch her breath or let the news sink in, I had no clue, but after a moment of stunned silence, she continued, "And surprise, surprise…investigators found a sizable rock next to the body, covered in blood. The police are hoping some of it was transferred from the assailant when he wielded the blows."

Blows? I mouthed to a wide-eyed Leah, as Decker prattled on.

"Anyway, they've kicked me from the scene, but while I'm here I'm gonna see what else I can find out about this homeless guy, maybe talk to a few of the others he hangs with, see if I can get a line on him or find out where he hangs during the day. I think we should plan to meet up at Destiny's later, once she opens for business. I'll probably be a few minutes behind you but just so we're on the same page, let's hold off on telling her about Cam, if you're cool with that?"

I was curious about her rationale but she seemed to have something on her mind or had a better understanding of the situation and the bar owner, so Anna agreed.

It was hard to fathom that Destiny's bar would be closed for business. I couldn't recall a time I'd felt the need to drink before noon. And suddenly, the only thing that made any sense was a good stiff cocktail—or maybe a few of them, so that I could forget the past twenty-four hours altogether.

Leah turned to Anna after Decker disconnected. "You're the boss, how do you want to play this?"

"We proceed as discussed with Decker." Anna gripped the wheel and punched the accelerator, propelling us forward as she shifted lanes and pressed through the sea of metal.

"What about Blaze?" I murmured.

Anna shrugged but continued to accelerate, whipping past a massive semi before tucking in front. "He's safer where he is. For now."

She must have caught something in my expression because after glancing at me, she added, "I don't think he had anything to do with Cam's death, but his actions as of late have been beyond reckless and childish." She released a breath, shaking her head. "And despite the fact I want nothing more than to throttle him right now, the truth is, the more time we spend focusing on him, the more time the real culprit is able to get away with murder. No, Blaze is a big boy and can take care of himself. Let's focus on what's important now."

I squeezed her arm. "Are you sure the two of you will be okay?"

She grasped my hand and offered a small smile as she gently squeezed back. "Don't worry about Blaze and me. Finding the killer has to be our priority, which means, for the time being, everything else needs to wait. Then, when all of this is over if there is no longer any 'two of you,' I think both of us will survive."

I nodded. "Okay, you got us out here—tell us—what we can do?"

Anna released a small, sad chuckle. "Alright, my minions. After we pay a visit to Destiny, your first mission, should you choose to accept it, is to get some of that darn stink off." She could barely contain a snort as she took in our exasperated looks.

She hadn't had much joy as of late so even the small outburst was welcome, even under the current state of affairs, as one snort turned into a baker's dozen.

"Hey, we've been confined in here with the d-o-g. You can't blame his odorousness on us," I protested, through my own bout of giggles as Leah sniffed herself.

Once the laughter subsided, Leah turned to Anna. "By the way, Decker filled us in on your…challenges…with Destiny."

Anna raised a brow, a quirk at the corner of her mouth. "Oh, did she now?"

"Uh huh. So, I guess what I'm asking is…on top of everything else, are you sure you're ready for this?"

Anna released a snort. "I think I can handle Diamond Destiny."

Leah looked at me and shrugged. I nodded in agreement. I wouldn't want to deal with either gal in a dark alley, much less a dive bar illuminated with beer lights.

We arrived at our destination around thirty minutes later and easily found a spot to park in the lot adjacent, which was sprinkled with only a handful of vehicles, though it was hard to tell if they were of current patrons or if they'd been left behind the prior night, while their owners slept off a raging hangover.

This time around, the bar was only slightly less smoke-filled than our last visit, though the smell of beer, liquor and pot still lingered, almost waiting to dive into our pores. A handful of day drinkers were settled at the bar but no one glanced in our direction as we entered—apparently, drinking beer takes a lot of focus.

Destiny was behind the bar, busy polishing off the tap handles and when she turned, a look of recognition crossed her face as she perused our little group.

Anna strode purposefully toward her. "Destiny."

"Anna Banana." Destiny broke into a wide smile and leaned over the bar, embracing our friend as Leah and I looked from one to the other.

"What the heck?" Leah murmured to me.

I shrugged. Decker's intel must have been off. Unfortunately, her track record hadn't been too stellar as of late.

"See you brought some friends." Destiny nodded, shaking our hands after releasing Anna. "Nice to see you gals again." She gestured for us to sit. "You guys ever get a line on Blaze?" It was all I could do to mask my expression as Anna offered her a noncommittal shrug. Destiny shook her head and smirked. "Cam never did make his way back, either. Maybe those two patched things up and went for a surf."

"We're moving forward while those two do whatever it is they do," Anna replied, bypassing the question as she shifted the conversation. "Anyway, we're trying to get some answers about the crew and these incidents that keep occurring and were wondering if you'd noticed anyone odd hanging around the bar lately—someone who seems off or just out of place?"

Destiny tossed her head back and hacked out a harsh laugh.

"Honey, this place is full of people who are off. In fact, it's nearly the only place in this flipping town that accommodates all types—most of us are out of place, wherever we go. At this joint, we don't discriminate as long as you mind your p's and q's and pay your bar tab without being asked twice."

She waved a hand at the patrons. "Most of the folks you'll see in here are regulars who have been coming here for years. Every once in a while, a few trendy types wander in and order their fancy Beverly Hills' cocktails. Some of 'em, we see again, some we don't. As long as the money's green, it makes no difference to me.

"I didn't hang a shingle to get myself featured in a magazine or on some tv show. We just serve cold drinks and offer a variety of entertainment options—staring at my hooters not being among them—as well as a lively selection of conversation." She looked around and nodded, smiling as she added, "It ain't much but in my book, Diamond Destiny's meets most people's needs."

Anna started to speak but paused when Destiny's attention strayed—her eyes widening as the door to the bar opened and she assessed the new arrival.

"Mmm…just what I needed…a cool drink of lemonade on a smoldering L.A. day."

I didn't point out it wasn't all that hot yet and got my own shocker as I recognized the tall, dark and disarmingly handsome stranger who had entered her establishment.

"Thought I'd find you…all of you…here." Mr. Cool Drink of Lemonade approached, giving us all long perusal, some more disapproving than others.

"What are you doing here, Abe?" Anna spun on her seat, crossing her arms.

"Frank called," he replied, his tone less than a cool drink of…whatever.

Anna snorted. "Fabulous. Must be part of that 'deduct it from his tab' business."

"Something like that." Abe squinted at Anna, as though seeing her for the first time. And frowned. "I'm disappointed that I didn't receive a courtesy follow-up after I so kindly offered his services, with no questions asked."

"Yeah, well, we've been kinda busy lately." Anna's response was not light on the snark. "Besides, let's not forget that while you gave me a number, it was Frank who offered his services. What do you have on the guy anyway?"

Abe shook his head. "Don't try to sidestep the issue, Anna. I still want to know why you've been holding out on us about your…situation."

Anna snorted and stepped closer to her colleague. "Whatever,

Abe. Like I said, have been kinda up to my craw lately with 'situations'." Anna let the emphatic finger gestures hang in the air.

"Uh-huh," he replied, glancing at each of us in turn, before adding, "says the gal hanging out in a bar in the middle of the day helping her cohorts tie one on."

I winced as Leah tried to hide a shot of cinnamon whiskey behind her back.

Anna scoffed, placing one hand on a hip. "For the record, no one's tying one on. We're here to conduct business with Destiny. Period."

Anna thumbed behind her, where Destiny stood, her focus still trained on Abe's…assets.

"Hers? Or yours?" Abe snorted.

Anna poked a finger into his chest. "We were actually having a little conversation here, before you took up all the air, Stanton. Do you mind?"

Abe shook his head, waved a hand. "Not at all. Go right ahead. I'll wait."

"Do you think you can at least contain yourself?" She asked.

"Yup. In fact, I'll just stand over here and observe. Quietly." He moved no more than a foot. "This should be plenty of room."

"You don't need to rush off on my account, Sunshine," Destiny interjected. "Come on, Anna Banana. Care to introduce me to your friend?"

Anna pressed a hand to her chest. "Goodness, where have my manners gone? Sorry D, figured you already knew this goon," Anna replied. "Meet Abe Stanton—one of my partners. His brother, Elijah, is probably lurking somewhere nearby."

"Mmm…mmm." Destiny's eyes were slits as they zoned in on her target, biting her lip suggestively as she added, "Must make for a hard day at work."

Leah glanced at me and rolled her eyes at the overt innuendo.

"If you only knew the half of it," Anna grumbled.

Her tone was not lost on Abe, who gave her a hard stare. "You do know I'm standing right here."

"That was *your* decision," Anna replied, swiveling the stool so that her back was to him. "Feel free to leave. Anytime."

Abe looked mildly amused. "Not a chance. Not after we left a job and raced all the way back here from Vegas. For you."

"Again, your choice—I didn't ask you to. In fact, feel free to turn and walk the way you came—all the way back to Vegas would be preferable." Anna paused to look at him before adding, "I won't even smirk when the door slaps you in the butt."

Destiny chuckled at Anna's forthrightness and when Leah opened her mouth to add her own ill-timed two-cents worth, I jabbed her in the side with a particularly sharp fingernail.

Abe stared at his partner. "From where I'm standing, it certainly seems as though you can use some help." He nodded at Leah and I. "Especially with this motley crew."

I glanced at Leah, who had a familiarly wicked spark in her eyes. I opened my mouth to offer commentary but Leah—whip-quick with the comebacks—used the opportunity to keep it simple.

"Well, perhaps you've been keeping that pretty head of yours in the smog for too long now, Stanton. 'cause from where this motley crew is standing—a little place we like to call the real world—your gal Anna here could be doing a lot worse. That's in case you hadn't noticed."

I bit my lip to stifle a snicker, somewhat impressed with her level of composure before she added, "Then again, excuse me for that oversight. It's quite apparent you hadn't noticed what's been going on in your own backyard. And, for the record, if it's the last thing I do, I'm gonna make you pay for that last comment. Over and over and over…"

Abe released a small snort, though his frown suggested he was anything but amused. "You keep promising that, Campbell, yet you're still playing footsy with Detective Vargas back in Phoenix."

Leah glared, while Anna tapped her toe and crossed her arms. "Anyway, getting back to it."

I shook my head when Leah opened her mouth and wisely elected to shut it, which Anna took as her cue to continue.

"A bit of final housekeeping, *Boss*. Need I remind you that the reason we're in this mess in the first place is that you and my fiancé decided to go behind my back and bring Decker in." She paused, scoffing when all he could do was offer her a blank stare. "Yeah, right. So I guess you'd didn't feel like you owed me the courtesy of letting me in on that little chat before you two bounced off to Vegas, did you?"

"Based on the crumbs I'd been given, it's not like it would have helped matters," Abe replied, pacing.

I noticed it made several of the patrons squirm in their seats. Truth be told—Abe Stanton could be a bit scary.

"In my defense, Blaze simply asked for a recommendation and I offered it. He didn't specify what the person would be doing or in what capacity he or she would be utilized, so I think your issue should reside with him." Abe glanced at Anna, who released an exasperated huff.

"Men are such idiots but if that only covered half of it, it still wouldn't be enough."

Abe frowned and opened his mouth to respond when a tall, tanned man in his late forties sauntered into the bar, frowning.

"What the hell, Destiny? There's a freakin' Ferrari parked in my spot—one of those stupid Malibu Barbie jobbies that probably belongs to some ditz who got lost on her way to the wine bar."

"That stupid Malibu Barbie car belongs to me, sir, and I'll be leaving after I've finished my business here, if that's all right with you?" Abe replied in his deep baritone, causing the man to start. "And for the record, it's black. Not pink."

After giving each other a head-to-toe perusal, I expected a full-out, Nicoh-style butt sniff. Instead, the man backed away and settled himself next to the other day drinkers, who had been amused enough to put their beers down to witness the impromptu entertainment.

"You a cop or something?" one of them called out.

"He's *something*, all right," Anna grumbled under her breath.

Abe ignored her but addressed the man. "No, sir, not a cop, but if you're gonna sit here and drink you may want to give the barkeep your keys. Looks like you're gonna be here for a while."

The man grunted as his compadres snickered, gesturing toward Destiny, who obligingly poured him a draft, her eyes never leaving Abe as she slid it down the bar and it was promptly retrieved before the man returned to his table and the peanut gallery resumed their previous activities.

"Just for the record, that's barkeep and owner." Her voice was low and smoldering as she offered a hand to Abe, who stepped forward and accepted it. "Diamond Destiny at your service, Abe Stallion—*whatever* the service."

I noticed Destiny held his hand a little longer than necessary as she slowly perused every inch. Abe didn't appear to mind and offered her the return favor, studying her physique, before meeting her eyes again.

"Nice to meet you, ma'am—and it's *Stanton*." Abe replied, his voice low.

"But of course it is." Destiny gave him a wink and blew him a kiss as she finally released his hand, but not before she stroked his palm, trailing his fingers to the tips.

Finally, Anna cleared her throat. "Now that we've gotten that awkward moment out of the way, can we please have our discussion with Destiny now? Time *is* of the essence."

Destiny broke her gaze and frowned. "Yes, of course. Bryce."

Anna proceeded and honestly, I was amazed at the ease with which she kept it together, knowing what she did about Cam.

"So, getting back to our conversation, you noted that no new patrons have started hanging around that have felt off or struck you as odd or out of place—at least not any more than normal. And there have been no altercations or incidents."

Destiny shook her head. "Nothing other than the random drunk jerk who makes the mistake of crossing my path and who is promptly ejected with a stern…warning to never, ever make that mistake again."

"I guess Blaze would be considered an exception, then," Anna replied dryly.

Destiny pinched her lips together before responding, "Sometimes, we're compelled to overlook things for family."

"Indeed we are." Anna glared at Abe, who focused his attention on our colorful surroundings.

"I really wish I had more to offer." Destiny paused to look at each of us, her expression and the delivery sincere.

I looked at Leah. "Video?" we both asked at the same time, having had some luck with that in the past.

Destiny eyes widened at our suggestion but nodded. "That, I might be able to help with. Might take me a bit but if you wouldn't be mind, I could shoot it to your cell phone later?" She paused before adding, "I'd hate to make you wait, especially considering your time constraints."

Anna nodded. "That definitely works for me."

"Cool," Destiny replied. "I'm hoping it won't take me too long but I want to make sure I find anything that could be relevant."

"We definitely appreciate that." Anna gave her a firm hug.

"You'll keep me posted," Destiny whispered. "No matter *what* you find."

Anna nodded as they embraced one final time before we

exited to the bar and headed to our respective vehicles, agreeing to meet the Stanton brothers at their office after we'd had a chance to freshen up.

Elijah was on the phone, seated in the passenger seat of the Ferrari, furiously scruffing his long sun-bleached waves. He paused to give us a brief wave but continued to frown as he listened to the caller.

Abe surveyed his brother, his mouth forming a tight line as he hopped into the driver's side and brought the exquisite piece of Italian machinery to life. Revving the engine, he slid his dark shades on, gave us a thumbs-up and without a word to his brother —still engrossed in his phone call—punched the gas.

Anna shook her head as she unlocked her SUV. "Those two."

"Double the trouble," Leah replied, snorting as they disappeared from view.

"Agreed," Anna mumbled, pulling the phone out of her back pocket and searching through her contacts. "Decker," she mouthed after selecting one.

It had not escaped our notice that the P.I. had not made it to the meet with Destiny, nor called to give us an update.

Anna left a brief message, letting her know that we'd finished at Destiny's and were returning to the Stanton's office after a quick stop at her condo, in case she wanted to meet us there.

She frowned as she added, "By the way, the Stantons are back. Just thought you'd appreciate a heads-up before you walked into a firestorm empty-handed. Then again, ignore that last bit. You probably never go anywhere unprepared. Anyway, shoot us a text letting us know you're on your way."

"Huh, something must have really gotten her attention. Maybe she nabbed a lead and wanted to tackle it before it got away," I replied.

"Like the witness at the beach managed to do," Leah murmured.

I nodded, batting at a damp strand of hair that had attached to my neck. "I don't know about the rest of you but I think I need a shower and some food." My stomach growled loudly just at the mention of nourishment. "Um, but not necessarily in that order," I added.

Leah and Anna looked at one another and chuckled.

"*We'll* be the judge of that," Leah replied.

"Touché," I grumbled.

Despite everything we'd encountered in the last twenty-four —wait, now thirty-six hours—it was always good to keep a sense of humor, no matter how short-lived it might be.

Sometimes you never know. It might just keep you alive.

CHAPTER SIXTEEN

Spit-shined and fed, we piled back into Anna's vehicle and headed to the Stanton's office. Nicoh was particularly grumpy after receiving a quick dusting of dry doggie shampoo following a brisk brush through to remove any potential fur puppies or mats. Of course, he sat with his back to me, even though his impromptu cleaning has been at Leah's insistence. It was either that or she'd threatened to attach a box of pine tree deodorizers to his collar.

Taking a short breather from the overwhelm of the previous day and the unknowns lurking in the future, we'd chatted as we shared a breakfast of peanut butter toast and iced caramel sauce lattes but the banter slipped away as we eased into traffic. Other than Nicoh's quiet snores, there was nothing but silence in the SUV, with each of us immersed in our thoughts.

While I had been to the city numerous times, something about death made it appear more dark and foreboding than it had before. Murder made it seem downright ominous and foreign. And evil. Even the haze that blanketed the city bolstered the aura of darkness as it followed us through the streets—ever present—keeping watch.

We tucked into the parking structure adjacent to the building and this time, opted to hike up the stairs to avoid another encounter with the security guard. Our story had been pretty thin, if not threadbare, the last time around and we didn't need to drag Anna into any more drama—certainly not our drama.

The Stantons were nowhere in sight when we arrived and Anna noted their assistants had the day off, so we had the office to ourselves. We used the time to help her clean the workspace, which looked no less shocking the second time around. It was certainly not something Anna needed Abe and Elijah to witness. And while I was certain they would be more than forgiving under the circumstances, I doubted Anna would be able to forgive herself.

With the three of us working in tandem, we made short work of the cleanup and had time to get a pot of coffee brewing, which served two purposes: 1) to supply of a jolt of caffeine to help us forge through whatever the rest of the day tossed at us and 2) to mask the stale smell that permeated the office, which had as of late served as both Anna's work and home.

We still hadn't heard a peep from Decker by the time Abe and Elijah arrived with a surprise in tow. Suddenly, the call that had commanded the younger Stanton's attention outside Destiny's bar made sense.

"Blaze!" Anna squealed, running to her fiancé and throwing her arms around him.

Blaze hugged her and despite having a puffy, split lip, managed to plant a kiss firmly on her mouth without wincing. He had cleaned up—gone were his shredded t-shirt and soiled cargo shorts—replaced with a fresh white linen dress shirt, pressed chinos and leather sandals. The only remnants of the previous evening were the tell-tale signs that marred his face and peeked from beneath the bandages spanning his knuckles and palms.

Abe cleared his throat and Anna pulled away from their passionate reunion, tucking a strand of hair behind her ear as her cheeks reddened. Blaze smiled and smoothed the hair back into place when it slipped, then tenderly grasped her hand before turning to address us, his face serious as he stopped to acknowledge us, meeting each of our eyes as he did.

"I don't quite have the words…" He paused, shaking his head before starting again, "I guess there is only one thing to say. I'm sorry for what you've had to go through—all of you—because of me. I also want to thank you for being here for Anna during this difficult time, especially when I wasn't."

He looked down at their clasped hands. "I owe you so much more than gratitude. And someday I hope that you can forgive me for my actions, though I realize it's more than I deserve, considering the way I have treated everyone the past several weeks—all the people I've managed to hurt. I will spend every last breath making it up to all of you but I know it will never, ever be enough."

He raised his head and looked at Anna, then at each of us in turn, his eyes filled with wetness. "So much irreparable…damage has been done. And while it weighs heavy on my soul, it doesn't begin to equate to what I deserve, which is an eternity of misery."

When he finished, I looked at the group, trying to identify each person's reaction and saw that it ran the gambit—a lot of arm crossing, brow furrowing, jaws grinding, head shaking and evil-eying—each of us measuring his words in our own way, while weeding out the gristle to get to the meat.

It had been quite a speech.

I had to wonder if that's all it had been—a speech—and, if so, for whose benefit?

"It's not your fault, Blaze," Anna said softly after an awkward period of silence. "You didn't harm anyone much less leave them for dead."

It was not the time to point out that someone hadn't merely *left* Cam for dead—they'd made sure of it.

Leah started to speak but Anna shook her head. I wondered if she was concerned about what information Blaze currently possessed.

Was it possible that he was not aware his friend had been murdered?

Leah caught Anna's gesture and used it as an opportunity to redirect the subject. "You're all dressed up." She nodded at his new digs.

Blaze rubbed his free hand through his hair. "Yeah, once these guys sprung me, I figured I was due."

"You're off the cop's radar, then?" Leah asked.

"For now." He turned to Abe and Elijah. "I'm so lucky you guys stepped in. Truly, I owe you everything."

Apparently, he didn't realize just how lucky he was…the drunk and disorderly didn't even begin to cover what he could soon be on the hook for, once law enforcement was able to build a case and found that witness. Even Terrence Edwards wouldn't be able to stop that train from coming.

Elijah shook his head, also catching Anna's look. "Honestly, it was all Decker. We just made a few calls, got the right people talking and expedited the process."

"So it was Decker you were talking to outside Diamond Destiny's?" I asked.

"Actually it was a cop friend of hers. Piedmont, I think he said his name was? Anyway, she came across some information and after putting two and two together, called in a personal favor— whatever that was all about—I have no idea, but Officer Piedmont helped coordinate Blaze's release."

I wondered what that information had entailed, noting neither Stanton hadn't offered to expound. "Where is Decker, anyway?"

"As far as we know, she's still at the beach, talking to people, trying to find any morsel that's out there so that we can figure out what happened, and why," Abe replied. "She was having a hard time with reception but was able to make contact with her cop friend, who was already down on the scene and encouraged him —he used a stronger term—to call and get us involved. She figured you guys probably already had your hands full at Destiny's."

He paused to look at Anna, who glanced up and met her bosses' eyes—and whatever passed between them, I wasn't sure, though perhaps it wasn't meant for anyone else. Eventually, Anna broke her gaze and returned to Blaze, who leaned against the door jamb, his eyes barely slits.

Anna coaxed him onto the couch and he obliged, plunking down on one side while pulling her down to join him on the other.

"Turns out that Decker did right by you after all, Dude," Elijah commented.

Blaze nodded, leaning into Anna for support. "I'll definitely need to make good on those mea culpas soon. I've really screwed things up where she's concerned. Honestly, I can't believe the crap I unleashed on her. She tried to warn me all along. If only I would have listened…maybe…"

Anna put a finger to his lips. "You can deal with all of that later. For now, why don't you tell us what happened after you and Cam left your condo, how you ended up at Destiny's and what in the hell could have possessed you to drink and drive—"

Blaze's eyes widened. "I wasn't drinking."

Leah snorted. "Then you must be a featherweight—getting drunk off the fumes—because you had an empty glass sitting in front of you when we arrived and frankly, you were not yourself. In fact, you were lucky Destiny didn't kick you out on your butt."

Blaze blinked. "I don't know what you are talking about. I swear I never drank anything. And…I don't recall seeing you at Destiny's. Did we talk?"

"You're kidding, right?" Leah wrinkled her brows and snorted. "You had some choice words for Decker and you weren't all that pleasant to Destiny, either. Even some of the regulars moved away from your barrage of insults and obscenities. You not only made an ass out of yourself. You made it worse by getting into your car and driving off." Blaze could only stare at her with his mouth hanging open as she continued, "You were essentially a loaded weapon, not only to the citizens of L.A. but to yourself. It was a miracle you made it all the way back to the beach."

Blaze frowned. "I don't remember any of that. I just remember wandering around the beach and stumbling into Decker. I'm not sure which one of us was more surprised."

"And you have no recollection of driving there?" Anna asked, frowning when Blaze shook his head. "What's the last thing you do remember?"

"I remember sitting at Destiny's waiting for Cam but he never showed. Things got kind of fuzzy after that."

He was waiting for Cam? I glanced around the room and noted the equally surprised looks.

"Why don't you start at the beginning, from when you left the accident scene," I suggested.

"You mean when we barely avoided being arrested and hauled to jail?" Blaze asked, blushing deeply when I shrugged, before adding, "Yeah, I kind of wish I could forget that part, too—especially Bryce's motorcycle accident." He blew out a breath.

"Just take your time," Anna urged. "We know it's going to be tough but it might help us track that missing time."

Blaze nodded. "The police released us with a stern lecture—barely a slap on the hand—once we promised to not return to the scene or cause any more trouble. It hurts to have to thank my dad's reputation for that one.

"Afterward, Cam pulled me aside and insisted I tell him what Bryce and I had been arguing about, so I filled him in on everything on our way back to town—from hiring Decker to investigate the threats, which pointed to Bryce, to the fight that forced him to storm off and get on that damn bike…" He paused, shaking his head.

"Of course, Cam was pissed at first, mostly because I hadn't trusted him enough to keep him in the loop but once he'd digested it, he admitted he'd been taking stock of the past several weeks and couldn't fault Decker for the conclusions she'd drawn. He'd started believing Bryce was involved in the threats and thought that I may have been complicit, too." Blaze chuckled but there was no humor behind it. "It's kind of ironic, don't you think? The perp has not only managed to throw a wrench into our lives, he's got us turning on each other. Anyway, Cam said that learning Decker's real purpose and where her investigation led sparked something."

"Did he say what?" I asked.

"No. He said he couldn't quite put his finger on it and wanted to revisit a few things he'd come across before he filled me in. When I pressed him on it, he said he just wasn't sure and that it would probably turn out to be nothing. It was the way he said it that gave me the impression he was actually hoping that it would turn out to be nothing."

"Strange," Leah murmured. "Then what happened?"

"We agreed that whoever had initiated the threats had also obtained access to each of us, our families and our homes and had likely been keeping an eye on us for a while. So as we made our way back to L.A., Cam and I decided to turn the tables on this jerk and toss him something to gnaw on so that we could divide and conquer, which would give Cam the time he needed to check out whatever he was going to check out without drawing attention to ourselves," he paused to gauge our expressions before adding, "any more attention, that is.

"So we did what we knew how to do. We created some drama. Only in this instance, we weren't doing it strictly for entertainment value. We were doing to gain back control of our lives." Blaze glanced at Anna, whose expression was stony as she shook her head.

"Anyway, we put our plan into motion once we arrived back at my condo, figuring he was watching. It consisted mostly of frat boy posturing-type stuff—yelling and stabbing fingers into each other's chest, that kind of thing. We were pretty sure he got a good show because several of the neighbors flipped their lights on and one of them threatened to hose us down, while another screamed something about releasing the hounds." Shaking his head as he released a weak laugh, he added, "She has a herd of Schnauzers—and while they are small, they are more stubborn than you'd expect—which would have been a serious deterrent to most. Not us, though.

"Still, we didn't need to risk getting arrested for the second time in one day. So we moved it inside, knowing our guy could probably still get a decent eyeful. We also kept up the trash talk, in case he had wired the place for sound.

"At first, it was kind of fun, most of my electronics need to be replaced anyway, but we quickly became worried about busting each other up enough without going overboard or giving the other one a serious injury.

"When Cam tried to goad me into punching him in the nose I refused—despite the fact he'd broken it at least a half a dozen times since we were kids doing stupid stuff. It wasn't easy to deliver that kind of pain—so he guzzled an energy drink, then bashed his face into the corner of the fireplace a couple of times."

Everyone winced, causing Blaze to nod.

"Believe me, it was hard to watch—and really, really messy— but we had to keep up the act, so we did a lot of cussing, throwing out death threats and other innuendos while I punched a hole in the wall and either kicked or turned over anything that would make the argument appear volatile. In hindsight, we were lucky that no one called the cops.

"After we'd trashed just about everything, including ourselves, and ensured we could both stand, Cam pretended to storm out and I made a panicked phone call to you."

Again, he peered at Anna. Her lips pressed into a thin line as he revealed their attempt at misdirection, while drawing her into the ruse.

"Anyway, we'd agreed to meet up at Destiny's afterward, once he'd looked into whatever it was he wanted to check, so that's where I headed shortly after Cam left, hoping this person would follow one of us…preferably me. In fact, Cam was sure that unless the guy had multiple sources watching us, I'd be the best bet."

"And you have no idea where he went?" Leah asked. "Cam, that is?"

Blaze shook his head. "No, he refused to tell me but I got the sense it wasn't that far, especially considering it was his idea to meet up at Destiny's. I waited for over an hour, even tried to call but got his voicemail and he still didn't show."

"When you were at the bar—before things went fuzzy—was there anything unusual that happened, anyone that struck you as odd?" I asked.

"Not really. I talked to a couple of regulars. Caught up with Destiny, who was surly as ever. Chatted with a fan who I hadn't seen for a while and wanted to buy me a shot, which I declined. Another dude tried to cop a cigarette off me and that's about it."

Anna sat up quickly. "A regular?"

Blaze started at the sudden movement, his eyes widening. "No, never saw him before, at Destiny's or anywhere else. Not that I looked swell but he looked a bit worse than I did and didn't smell all that hot either. If I would have thought Destiny had allowed it, I would have considered him to be a transient."

"Describe him," I commanded. "What did he look like?"

"Geez, AJ, I just told you. He was a bit haggard. He'd definitely seen better days. You know the type."

I shook my head. "No, Blaze, I need you to focus. Be specific. What was he wearing? How tall was he? What kind of build did he have? What color was his hair? His eyes? Did he have an accent?"

"You're kidding me, right?" Blaze opened his hands to me before looking around the room. "You're seriously grilling me about some random dude because he asked for a smoke?"

"No, Blaze," I replied. "I want you to describe him, not because he was looking for a cigarette but because there was a man who claims to have seen you down at the beach—one who may have insights to your missing time."

Blaze looked at me, his eyes wide. "Really?" I nodded. "Okay, from what I can remember, he had dirty blonde hair, you know, kind of like Kurt Cobain. His build was thin but he seemed strong. I'd probably put him at six foot or six foot one. I couldn't see his eyes through all the hair. Even though he spoke low, there was a slight Southern accent. He was also tan. Not the fake kind."

"What was he wearing? Did he have any tattoos or scars?" Leah asked, sitting on her haunches.

"Mmm…no, long sleeve shirt, one of those running types. It was dark blue or black and I think he was wearing basketball shorts of the same color. Honestly, I didn't look at his feet." Leah and Anna and I exchanged glances. "Come on! I am not part of the shoe crew. I would barely know the difference between a sandal and a flip-flop. But seriously, do you really think it could be the same dude?"

Leah shrugged, causing Blaze to frown, but she persisted. "After this guy asked you for a cigarette, what happened?"

"Nothing happened," he replied. "I told you, I just sat there, waiting for Cam."

"And you had nothing to drink?" she prompted.

"No alcohol, no."

Anna caught his chin. "You had something."

Blaze raised his hands. "Alright, you caught me. I had a club soda and lime."

"In a glass," Anna prompted.

He squinted at her. "Yes, they're normally served in a glass. Where are you gals going with this?"

"Blaze, you seem to remember everything about the evening —as clear as that damn glass—right up to the point in the evening where the dude you didn't recognize asked you for a cigarette. Can we agree on that?" I asked and when Blaze nodded I added, "Was he sitting next to you at the bar for any length of time?"

"No, he never sat down next to me, he just tapped me on the shoulder—I think I was talking to Destiny or maybe her backup— and then he went away when I told him I had none, so I just figured he copped one from someone else. And then..." Blaze squinted.

"You blanked out?" Leah asked.

"Well, now that I think about it, it's the first time I can't remember...anything." He glanced at us. "What are you thinking?"

"I'm thinking," Anna replied, looking around the room before continuing, taking account of what she saw in each of our faces. "We're all thinking—whether you want to believe it—is that someone put something in your soda."

Blaze appeared genuinely surprised, first glancing at his fiancé before looking at the rest of our faces. "You really think that someone drugged me?" When we nodded, he added, "For what purpose, exactly?"

"So he could get you where he wanted you, at the very spot he needed you," Leah replied.

Blaze opened his mouth, closed it.

He sat for a moment before commenting. "And so that he could say he saw me there."

Leah nodded. "And so that, if it served his greater purpose—or the purpose of whoever it is he works for—he could blame a murder on you if he needed to."

It was as though the air left the room. Anna looked at Leah, whose mouth formed an "o" as she realized the line she had crossed. There was no going back.

"What are you saying…who's murder? Did they find Bryce?" Blaze searched our faces, his eyes wide and his speech rapid.

"When Decker found you at the beach, she got you into her vehicle and was still following up on leads. Apparently, you were sleeping it off when the homeless guy spotted you, which is when all hell broke loose," Abe replied. "Does any of this sound familiar?"

"Seriously?" Blaze shook his head. "I don't remember squat after Destiny's. I'm honestly surprised I didn't end up with a tattoo on my face or sporting a Mohawk. I woke up in a room with not much more than a bed, still pretty out of it, so I wasn't sure if I'd been arrested or was in a hospital. I had barely started asking questions when these guys showed up to spring me."

Anna turned toward the Stanton's. "And the two of you didn't assist him in filling in the blanks?"

It wasn't an accusation, merely a clarification.

Both frowned and shook their heads, while Blaze surveyed each of our faces.

"What am I missing here?"

"This witness—the homeless guy Decker is trying to track down—claimed to have seen you in an altercation at the beach," Leah replied.

Blaze snorted. "Well, that's choice. If I could barely find my butt with my own hands, how could I have managed to get myself to the beach, much less gotten into a fight with a complete stranger?"

"Not a stranger, Blaze," Anna replied, her voice low. "Cam."

"I was seen fighting with Cam? At the beach?" Blaze's eyes widened.

Anna shook her head. "It's worse than that, Blaze. The witness claimed to have seen you hit Cam and when he fell, you left him for dead."

Blaze stood, nearly knocking Anna off the couch in the process. "What are you saying? Where is he?" He gripped her shoulders, forcing her to stand. "Where is Cam, Anna?"

"I'm sorry, Blaze." A tear slid down her face. "Cam's dead."

CHAPTER SEVENTEEN

"Blaze, come on, man. You need to ease up on her." Abe stepped toward him, placing a hand on his shoulder until Blaze released his grip on his fiancé, pressing his fists to his eyes as he did.

Anna attempted to pull him into a tight embrace. "I am so sorry, Blaze."

"You have to be wrong." Blaze pushed away, holding a hand up and shaking his head as he began pacing the room. "They have to be wrong."

"Blaze, I'm afraid what she said is true. Decker was the one who identified him at the beach," Elijah replied, causing Blaze to stop.

"How?" Blazed demanded. "*How* did he die?"

"The witness placed two men at the beach having a heated argument, followed by a physical altercation. During this altercation, one man—the witness later claimed was you—struck the other man hard enough to cause him to fall. The witness went on to claim that the first man stood over the fallen man, who was not moving, and leaned down—he assumed to check a pulse—before racing away from the scene."

"So this witness, he's saying I beat Cam to death?" Blaze's asked, squinting at Elijah. "As in…used my fists?"

Elijah shrugged. "Hard to say what actually killed Cam. A sharp, bloodied rock was near the body…near Cam. Whether he was struck with it or hit his head on it when he stumbled from the blow of a fist has yet to be determined, pending an investigation…blah, blah, blah." He waved his hands in a circular motion to suggest the typical investigation rhetoric.

Blaze snorted. "But Decker thinks it was the prior, doesn't she?" When Elijah said nothing, Blaze strode up to him, until they were eye to eye. "Does she…believe I did this?"

Elijah used a single finger, pressing it into Blaze's chest until the other man took a step back before responding, "No, I don't think Decker believes you were involved. Directly, anyway."

"Well, that's certainly a relief." Blaze threw his hands up, his voice edged with sarcasm. "And now we'll never know what Cam was looking for, though maybe that's why he was at the beach."

Elijah's phone rang. After checking the screen, he excused himself. In his absence, we continued to gently prod Blaze, hoping to spark something about the missing hours but nothing substantial came out of it by the time Elijah returned, a look of concern spanning his face.

"It's confirmed. Blaze had Rohypnol in his system. Based upon the level still in his blood when he was tested, he wouldn't have been in any condition to have been in a physical altercation during the timeframe they believe Cam was murdered. Also, a majority of the blood on his clothes and hands was his own, which doesn't support the evidence at the scene or the witness' account." Before we could ask who had so generously supplied this information, he added, "Friend of mine at the department gave me the heads up."

"Does this mean he's in the clear?" Leah asked.

Elijah shrugged. "It will probably ease the pressure on him—for Cam's murder, anyway."

Blaze frowned, crossing his arms. "They still think I am responsible for my best friend's motorcycle accident?"

"Until a body shows up, they'll continue looking at everyone he was associated with," Abe responded for his brother, who nodded.

Blaze shook his head. "And what happens if his body never turns up? Unless they get something definitive from the accident site or the bike, I'll never be completely off their radar."

"Probably true," Abe replied, causing Blaze's frown to deepen. "It's not like they have the resources to continue actively pursuing a search."

Blaze nodded, huffing out a long breath. "But I know someone who does."

"Blaze—no." Anna went to his side, grabbing his arm. "You can't get your father involved. You know what kind of circus he'll create. He'll turn it around so it's all about him and we'll never uncover who's behind this. Cam…and Bryce will never get the justice they are due. Please, think about this."

Blaze raised his hands, puffed out a breath. "What else can we do? One of my friends is dead. The other is missing and likely dead. I can't bear to think about, much less risk anything happening to you."

Anna released his arm, looking down. "About that."

Blaze stared at her. "What? What aren't you telling me?"

We managed to cop a temporary break when Anna's phone rang—none of us looked forward to explaining how we'd barely avoided having our body parts scattered up and down his street.

Anna waved her phone. "It's Destiny. I have to get this."

Blaze shook his head, looking from one of us to the next but we remained silent as she took the call, noting that her frown increased as she listened to the bar owner.

"You sure?" she asked, before releasing a long breath. "Okay, I appreciate you letting me know. Keep us posted if anything turns up." She stared at her phone for a long moment after ending the call. "Well, that was a bust. Destiny's got nothing for us."

"So she didn't see anything of value on the video?" Leah asked before mumbling, "I wish she would have allowed us to be the judge of that."

I nodded, recalling that Destiny had agreed to let us see the recording.

Blaze perked up, eyes wide as he stared at his fiancé. "What video?"

"The one from the bar's security system," I replied for Anna, who was nibbling on a nail, her brows furrowed. "We asked Destiny to pull the footage from last night."

"Video that shows someone spiking my beverage?" Blaze's tone was hopeful.

Anna tossed her phone on the desk. "It probably could have. Unfortunately, the laptop it was stored on was stolen from behind the bar. Destiny was dumbfounded, as it was pretty well hidden—under a case of Jack Daniel's or something—and only a handful of her employees knew about it. She vouched for all of them—most of them have worked for her since she opened—one is a cousin and another is such a technophobe he would've broken out in a rash if someone even mentioned the word 'laptop,' so handling it would have been like contracting the plague."

"Crap. When was the last time she'd seen it?" I asked.

Anna paced the floor. "Destiny didn't recall, specifically, though she admitted it had been more a couple of days since she'd checked it. She asked her employees and they confirmed the same."

Abe groaned. "You've got to be kidding me. So it could have been stolen last night."

"Or any time prior, to prevent any evidence being recorded," I added.

"This guy just keeps throwing punches, doesn't he?" Anna replied.

"He is certainly well prepared and has covered all the bases, dotted all of the i's, crossed all of the t's," I grumbled.

Leah shook her head. "He didn't get all of the i's—we're still alive."

"About that." Blaze had been listening to our banter and quickly caught the reference, as well as his fiancé's reaction.

Trying to override her gaff, Leah elected to ignore him. "You know, this guy is pretty sharp. Maybe he had Destiny under surveillance, too."

I nodded. "Leah's right. If Cam was being watched, we have to assume Destiny was, too, considering he typically stayed at her apartment."

"Do you think she's in trouble?" Blaze asked, his eyes widened.

"It's hard to say, but with Cam's death and the video gone, she may not even be on his radar. Then, on the other hand, considering we have no idea about his motivation, much less his end game, we should probably call her and tell her to watch her back."

Everyone nodded but something told me Diamond Destiny could take care of herself, whatever the threat.

CHAPTER EIGHTEEN

"Why does it feel like we're always a step behind?" Leah asked of no one as she tugged her hair.

"We're more than a step behind," Anna grumbled, shoving papers across the desk so she could plop down on the corner.

"You're looking at this from the wrong angle." I shook my head, and suddenly five pairs of eyes were trained on me—unnerving, to say the least. "We have one thing the perp doesn't." I received several doubtful looks and more than a few frowny faces. "Come on, guys—we still have one ace in the hole."

Anna nodded, a small smirk forming at the corner of her mouth. "Decker."

Leah joined in, her eyes bright as she used her hands to gesture while talking. "We need to share what we've learned from Blaze. Perhaps she's come across something that can help us find what Cam was looking for and why he was at the beach."

"I'd also like to know more about this dude that identified me," Blaze growled. "If not get my hands on him."

Abe nodded. "If anyone can get a line on him, it's Decker." He glanced at us. "I think her father was the only person I've ever met that was more tenacious than she is."

"You knew him?" I asked.

"We did." Abe's expression was unreadable.

"And?" Leah prompted.

"It's a story for another day," was the reply, ending the conversation. "So, are we calling Decker, or what?" Abe looked at Anna.

"Sure thing, Boss," she replied as she collected her phone from the desk.

"On speakerphone, please," the elder Stanton prompted.

"As you wish," Anna replied, punching a number in her contact list.

Decker answered on the first ring and once everyone offered a quick hello, she added, "Glad to hear you made it out, Blaze."

"From what I hear, I have you to thank for that, Decker."

"I'll remember that when tallying your bill." She hacked out a harsh laugh. "You have any trouble, Stanton?"

"Nope, your cop friend did you a solid," Elijah replied. When Decker grunted, he added, "Of course, none of us could have done it without your intel. Good work."

"It's what I do…or at least what I try to do," she replied. "You called me. You got something?"

"We do," Elijah replied, filling Decker in on everything that had transpired after she and Blaze had parted ways, ending with, "According to Blaze, Cam thought he had a line on whatever this dude was after—it would have made sense that he was at the beach if it had to do with their current project."

Decker was silent until he finished. "Interesting. A few things just clicked into place. Or at least make a bit more sense."

Chatter filled the room as everyone tossed questions at her. Finally, a loud whistle emitted over the line.

"Come on, guys, there's a half dozen of you and only one of me. And, believe me, while I can certainly handle all of you and kick your butts, I can't possibly answer all of you at once, nor make sense of your jabbering." The group went into a collective silent mode, causing her to snort. "I think it's best if I take the lead here and tell you what I know. From there, we can wrap it up with a little Q&A. Sound good?" Decker chuckled at the grumbled responses or lack thereof. "Cool. Let's begin."

All of us perched in various locations of the Stanton's office —some of us on couches or chairs, others remained standing. I sat on the floor and stroked Nicoh's velvety ears, listening to him sleep. Within seconds, everyone was within clear earshot of Anna's cell phone, eagerly leaning forward. I hoped Anna's battery was charged because I was betting this conversation was gonna be a doozy.

"First, let's talk about the witness who claimed to have seen Blaze fighting with Cam."

"Only later to finger me while I was passed out on the front seat of your vehicle," Blaze growled, pinching his lip between his forefinger and thumb.

"I think we can agree his account was suspect," Decker replied, "and convenient."

Abe nodded to no one in particular. "It would be nice to have something concrete to validate our suspicions—our instincts don't seem to be getting us too far as of late."

"Then try this on for size," Decker replied. "I talked to the officer who took the witness' statement—turns out he provided a false name and because he had no address—other than the beach —nothing about him could be verified."

"I don't see how that helps us," Abe grumbled.

"Hang on to your tighty-whiteys, Stanton, I'm getting there." Despite the jest, Decker sounded no more amused than I was. "Let's get back to the discussion of our homeless dude whose whereabouts are currently unknown."

I frowned. Decker certainly knew how to drive a negative point home.

As if sensing the discontent on the other side of the connection, she added, "According to the beach cops, he's not a regular. The other homeless that frequent the area said the same thing and while they knew who I was talking about, they suggested he'd only been around a few times over the past couple months. All of them mentioned he wasn't really the friendly sort, didn't engage much and was never seen hanging around with anyone. In fact, they seemed to feel as though something was off about him."

"Off, as in he's a weirdo?" Leah asked.

"No," Decker replied. "Off as in he didn't belong."

"You did just say he was new to the area," Elijah suggested. "He could have moved from another beach."

"Maybe, but the vibe I got from the locals was that he wasn't all that he seemed—meaning that while he looked and acted the part, he wasn't actually one of them."

I glanced at Leah, who raised a brow and nodded. *Now* we were getting somewhere.

"For one, they said he was too clean. Looked like he had worked too hard to appear worn down and beaten by life, and instead ended up looking like he'd just come from one of those mod runway shows—platinum bedhead, big eyes, sunken cheeks, deep tan and thin build." Decker hesitated. "Okay, I added that runway part but they said he just didn't fit the usual mold. Plus, more than one of them commented that his teeth were ultra-white and his shoes were trendy ones worn by skateboarders."

"I suppose there's zero chance he stole them off someone?" Anna suggested.

"Only if he stole a watch, too," Decker replied. "And from what they described, it sounded pricey. Wears it on his right arm, backward."

"I wonder why he allowed them to get so close, if he wasn't really supposed to be there or didn't want to be found out," I murmured.

"That's been bothering me, too," Decker responded. "The locals mentioned the other thing that seemed off about him was his demeanor. He was typically stand-offish but then on random occasions, would engage with them to swap cigarettes for water or a beer or something. And while he wasn't overly talkative, he did ask a few of them what they thought about the filming that was going on and would get pissed whenever someone said anything resembling a positive response.

"Some of them thought he was undercover, working for some sort of environmental group and avoided him after that," Decker replied. "And honestly, if this guy is associated with our perp, I don't know that I would blame them."

"When was the last time they remembered talking to or seeing him?" Anna asked.

"Here's the thing—one old man, who said his name was Bunyan, like the lumberjack, not the foot condition, not only saw our witness, he talked to him."

"Interesting," Abe replied. "And just what did this Bunyan have to say?"

"Our witness asked Bunyan if he'd seen that guy from extreme sports videos milling about. Description sounded an awful lot like you, Blaze," Decker replied, drawing a frown from him. "Anyway, Bunyan had a good laugh about it, told our witness 'yeah, sure, like I can get a good satellite signal from under the pier.' Our guy got feisty so Bunyan told him to piss off and the dude grabbed him by the shirt and roughed him up a bit. Bunyan was embarrassed to reveal he had thrown in the towel because the guy was not only younger, but a lot more physically fit. After that, Bunyan confessed that he hadn't seen whatever the dude was rambling about, at which point, he tossed Bunyan to the ground and stormed off. He showed me some bruises but who knows."

"Was Bunyan able to tell you when this whole shakedown supposedly occurred?" I asked.

"Here's the rub. A short time before our witness claims to have seen Blaze conking Cam on the melon and running up the beach."

"Nothing like another coincidence," Leah replied, frowning.

Something churned in my brain. "This Bunyan guy got up close and personal with our witness—did he remember any specific, scars, tattoos, a smell? Or did any of the others remember anything?"

Decker replied. "You know, at first, I thought I struck out on that. A few of them said he looked familiar but that they couldn't place him. Then again, they thought I looked familiar. One claimed I was his sister. Another thought he'd been married to me in a former life. You get the drift. But Bunyan...he was a bit sharper than most. He said that while he hadn't seen him before, he also said he looked..." Decker paused to snort, "waxy and thought maybe he was one of those Hollywood types."

"Waxy, as in plastic surgery?" Leah asked, raising a brow.

"He wasn't sure. He just said that while the black, cruel eyes spoke the truth, everything else seemed like a painting...almost surreal," Decker replied.

"He could have been purposely trying to mask his appearance with makeup or something," I suggested. "Anything else, Decker?"

"Said the guy smelled like cinnamon...maybe gum? And he had a tattoo, written in script, across the inside of his forearm. But he couldn't read it...it wasn't in English."

Elijah snorted. "Fabulous. We've got a witness who chews gum, may or may not wear makeup, has expensive taste in watches, likes a good pair of board shoes and has a tattoo. Pretty much describes half the population of California."

"Hey, don't poke the messenger." Decker's voice came across the connection in a low rumble, almost a growl.

Elijah started to respond when Leah interjected, "At least we've confirmed that our guy was definitely interested in Blaze and the film production."

"She's right," Decker replied. "Hang on for a second, I'm getting a text."

We made small talk while she placed us on hold. It was daunting, having to base an investigation on a mysterious stranger that may or may not have been homeless. One thing was for sure—he was currently lying low. Again, those damn shadows.

Decker dropped back into the conversation. "Alright, I may have something. Blaze, I'm shooting an image to your phone."

As his phone beeped, Blaze scanned through the texts and peered at the screen. "Who is it, Decker?"

"According to Bunyan, it's a decent likeness of our guy," Decker replied. "He's actually a pretty good artist and offered to draw it for me. I gave him a hundred bucks and called my officer friend to take his statement and collect the sketch. I asked him to text it to me when Bunyan finished."

"Wow, the guy who sketched this is homeless?" Blaze said as he continued to stare at the image as we huddled around. "This is better than some of the stuff in the museums Anna drags me to."

The quiver at the corner Anna's mouth suggested she didn't mind the dig. She did, however, snatch the phone from her fiancé's hand so the rest of us could take a peek.

The man in the sketch had longish hair and from the way it was drawn, it appeared as though it was bleached by the sun, though it could have been a wig or a convincing set of extensions. His face was angular, ending with a cleft in his chin, which was covered with a thin coating of facial hair. His nose was long and straight in a Roman type formation. But it was his eyes that drew you in—piercing and cold. Perhaps it was the artist's rendering, but they felt as though they were staring through you, directly into your soul.

Anna broke my concentration as she handed the phone back to Blaze. "Do you recognize him?"

Blaze looked at it again, nodding after a long moment. "I think I might have seen this guy."

"From the beach?" Anna leaned in, her eyes wide.

"Not the beach." He shook his head, tapping on the screen. "But he looks a lot like the dude who was trying to bum a cigarette at Destiny's."

There was a collective moment of silence as we all peered at the screen again.

Abe was the first to speak. "If he's been watching you at the beach, he could have also been the one who drugged your soda."

"You really think he's one and the same?" Blaze asked, still staring at the face—and the eyes that stared back.

"It's a definite possibility," Decker replied. After a moment, she added, "If so, he could have also driven your car and deposited both you and it at the beach."

Blaze frowned. "I don't remember any of that."

"It's not your fault, man," Elijah patted him on the back. "Stuff was strong enough to prevent an elephant from remembering."

"Not very comforting," Blaze murmured. "It seems stupid to ask at a time like this, but where did my car end up, anyway?"

Decker immediately piped up, "I have a friend bringing it back to the city once the investigators are done with it."

Blaze frowned and looked to the rest of us. "Why are they looking at my car?"

Decker sighed and I wondered if she regretted stepping in so quickly. Then again, the gal was big on transparency.

"Because it was parked right next to Cam's. At the beach."

Elijah shook his head. "This guy pulls out all the stops, doesn't he? Calculated."

"Too calculated, if you ask me," Anna grumbled.

"Did they find anything in either of the cars?" Abe asked.

"So far, no, Blaze's was clean—maybe a bit too clean—perp did a thorough job," Decker replied. "Cam's was more like you would have expected—multiple sets of prints, including Cam's, were found."

Blaze shrugged. "Yeah, that makes sense. All of us, Tate, Cam, Bryce—even you, Decker—either drove or rode in it at some point." He waited for Decker's grumbled response before adding, "Anyway, thanks for taking care of my car, Decker. Not to mention, following up with law enforcement and calling in favors like you have. I've been a real jerk lately and I owe you big time."

Decker snorted. "Sure, Kid. Like I said before, I'll add it to my bill." When Blaze snickered, she changed the subject, hitting on a more serious note. "Moving on to Cam. There's really no easy way to put it but it's been confirmed—he died from the head injury—an unfortunate side effect of being beaned by a sizable rock."

"It is possible he fell during the altercation and hit his head on the rock after the fact?" Anna asked as she chewed on a nail.

"No, based upon the position of the body, which was face down, they believe the perpetrator approached from behind and delivered the death blow. It would have been difficult for him to survive based upon the size of the hole in his skull," Decker blew out a breath before continuing, "I'm not trying to be callous, but had he survived, he would have likely been in a permanent vegetative state. And, I don't know about you, but I certainly wouldn't have wanted that for myself."

Blaze fisted his hands at his sides. "Cam wouldn't have

wanted to live like that, either. I know I wouldn't. And I'm pretty sure I knew my friend."

Abe nodded absently. "Any ideas how it occurred….the knockdown, that is?"

Decker huffed out a breath. "Best guess? It appears as though he was in a squatted position when the perp snuck up and brained him with the rock. Cam fell forward and that's all she wrote."

"Any footprints leading away?" Elijah asked.

"Nah, by the time anyone arrived on the scene—anyone that was there in an official capacity, that is, they'd all been washed away. Or tromped over." Another collective sigh of disappointment was expelled before Decker added, "On a strange side note, Cam had an empty vial clenched in his hand and another one filled with liquid in his pocket when they found him."

We looked at one another then at Blaze, who shrugged. Finally, Leah asked, "What the heck was in it?"

"According to the tech who collected them at the scene— another pal of mine—guessed it was ocean water but is running some tests to confirm. Whatever it was, Cam must have felt it was important."

"Any idea what he might have looking for?" Anna asked, turning toward her fiancé.

Blaze shook his head. "I honestly don't know but of all of my guys, Cam was the most intuitive. Decker's right—if he thought something was important, it was."

"Speaking of the crew, I hope you don't mind but I talked to most of them." I noticed Decker wasn't really asking for Blaze's approval as she added, "The cat's out the bag where I'm concerned. I expected to receive some pushback but all of them were eager to help because the accidents have transitioned into something far more serious. Now we're talking about people's lives. You've got a good crew, Blaze.

"Anyway, a few recalled a few days where Cam had seemed

off—both moody and sullen. The crew gave him a bunch of crap and he eventually revealed that he'd noticed a couple of people lingering a bit too much during filming, sometimes even screwing with his shots, which he felt was done intentionally. Finally, he decided to just go ask them to move but when he got within range, they raced off."

Blaze nodded this time. "This is starting to sound familiar. Keep going."

"Well, he mentioned noticing them again on another day—not that long after—you guys moved up the beach but this time they weren't interfering with the shot. Instead, they were intently watching the crew. Cam said he typically wouldn't have noticed but something caught his eye. Whether it was something about the person, specifically, or something else, I don't know. It may just have been something that seemed odd. Or been familiar. But unfortunately, now we'll never know."

Something occurred to me. "Hold on, Decker. Maybe we will." I turned to Blaze. "It's possible that you have whoever it was on film? Maybe even doing whatever it was that Cam saw?"

Blaze nodded. "Sure, we'd shoot for hours, clean it up later. Our editing guy is the best so he isn't cheap. We tried to tackle any issues to minimize the edits needed later, which is probably why Cam wanted to approach them—to encourage them to move along. Usually, once we explained the nature of what we were doing and why we were doing it, people were happy to comply. Some even offered to help if they could.

"I'm still racking my brain trying to remember this particular instance, though it sounds like it stood out to Cam because of the reaction he received. Anyway, long answer to a short question—it would have been recorded but if it was filmed prior to the fire in the storage unit then we're out of luck. We ended up having to reshoot a lot of the scenes."

"That sounds…expensive," Leah replied.

"It is, which is why I've been careful to make sure all of the costs have been out of pocket—err, my pocket." When he caught our questioning looks, he added, "Don't worry, I'm not dipping into my trust fund. Everything I've put into this was taken from my portion of the proceeds from the extreme sports series and its merchandising."

"Nice," Abe nodded. "How does that work, then, dividing up the profits after the dispensing the money you've set aside for the charity?"

"We're all equal partners," Blaze replied.

"But you were the only one putting in money?" Leah asked.

"Yeah, some of the guys wanted to toss some money in, but I had more than enough to cover it. Besides, after their loyalty all those years—a lot of them pretty lean—I figured it was the least I could do."

"Do you expect sizable profits from the documentary, once it's been released?" Elijah asked.

Blaze shrugged. "To be honest…no. It's always been more about getting the word out—about preserving the environment, our beaches and the wildlife that inhabits it." He smiled at Anna, who reached out and clasped his hand.

"Plus, the potential for future projects," Anna added. "Think Sundance Film Festival."

"So, getting back to the film," Blaze replied, after giving her a peck on the cheek, causing her to turn a bright shade of pink. "I can't remember when it occurred, but it's likely that the footage is gone."

"Maybe," Decker murmured.

"What are you thinking, Decker?" Abe asked, squinting at the phone.

"I need to check something, though it'll probably turn out to be nothing." Before we could ask her for details, she added, "Got to put you on hold—it's my friend from the lab.

He's got initial results on the water samples from Cam's pocket."

"That was fast," Leah replied dryly, once Decker put us on hold.

I nodded. It was clear that Decker, for whatever reason, was suddenly dodging us.

"She must have good friends."

"Or a lot of friends that owe her favors," Leah grumbled.

"She does," Abe replied, causing all heads to turn in his direction, "have a lot of friends in high places. Like her dad, she has a knack for collecting people in all areas and walks of life that are happy to do her favors or put themselves on the line for her. There's just something about her that draws people in."

Decker seemed to travel light in the warm fuzzy department. Then again, I'd only known her for a day and despite her lone wolf persona, she had been fiercely loyal and true to her word. And downright tenacious, if the situation warranted it.

"Well, that was…interesting." We heard rustling as Decker popped back into the conversation. "I had to jot down some of the more technical terms but according to my pal at the lab, the vials found on Cam contained ocean water, along with high levels of a toxin that I can't even begin to pronounce, though I can tell you it has about twenty-five syllables and a lot of consonants in a row.

"Anyway, in high doses, it could impact the quality of the water and disrupt the entire ecosystem, which could pose an imminent threat to any marine or wildlife in its wake." Decker paused before adding, "This is just my take on what the lab guy told me—don't quote me, cause I don't know what the hell I'm talking about."

"Imminent threat…meaning it could kill them?" Anna asked.

More shuffling paper ensued. I envisioned Decker thumbing through her notes. "Or stave off future populations, essentially depleting the number so severely there would be fewer and fewer numbers left to reproduce," was the grim response.

"So they would eventually die off," I confirmed.

"Because of the small number already present, yes. And unless they were able to identify and eradicate the source, they would need to be moved to a more suitable location or—"

"Or risk losing the species altogether," Abe replied, his tone somber.

"Yes," Decker replied, her voice equally dour over the connection.

"Is there any other way this toxin could have made its way into the water?" Leah asked.

Elijah glanced over his shoulder at her, squinting. "What… like a kid peeing in the pool?"

I couldn't tell if he was being serious, though Decker responded as though she either hadn't noticed or just didn't care. "There's no reason for it being there, which is why my friend is going to collect additional samples from the beach. Of course, the more testing that is required the longer it will take to get answers."

"Longer is not really something that helps us." Blaze sat as he rubbed his eyes and mussed his hair.

"No, but the answers aren't preventing us from moving forward either," Decker replied.

"Right." Abe stood up, rubbing his hands together and stretching his muscles. "Tell us what you'd like us to do, Decker."

"If you could, I'd appreciate it if you would follow up on the status of Bryce's accident and see if they've come up with anything else. I've exhausted all the resources I have, so it might benefit it us if we go at it from a different angle.

"Also, talk to your bomb dude, see if he has any more thoughts and if you have time, I'll shoot you the list of the investors interested in that land. Nothing popped the first time but a lot has happened and maybe we can scare some of them out of their rat holes to see if anything strikes you as suspicious. You could always sic the bomb guy on 'em if you needed to."

It seemed to me as though someone was trying to keep us occupied, so she could pursue her own leads without interference.

I shuddered, wondering if she'd been reading my mind when she added, "I know it all seems like senseless busy work but I have something that I need to confirm personally, so any headway you can make in the meantime will definitely help."

"It's a little late to be holding it so close to the vest, don't you think?" I was glad Abe had been the one to pose the question.

Decker grunted. "Not so much, Stanton—just a hunch and a loose one at best. No need to get anyone's hopes up until I take a look-see." When she was met with a resounding silence, she huffed. "Listen, I'm not trying to be cagey, I just don't want you putting stock into something that's probably nothing more than another addition to the crap pile."

"Fine, Decker," Abe replied, crossing his arms as he leaned toward the phone. "If you need backup…"

"When I do, you'll be the first to know."

Abe shook his head, lifting his eyes toward the ceiling. "Be safe Decker. There's evil lurking in the shadows."

"The shadows I can handle, it's the evil standing in plain sight that I worry about."

CHAPTER NINETEEN

No one had noticed that Blaze had slipped out until he shuffled back into the room, hands shoved into his pockets, drawing curious looks from the group. When Anna gasped, we realized the answer resided with the elder gentleman who sauntered in directly behind, scrunching his refined nose as he took stock of the surroundings.

"Mr. Edwards." Anna quickly gained her composure, stepping toward the newcomer and embracing him in an awkward hug followed by a series of air kisses. As she attempted to back away, he continued to clutch her hand, while casting a sneer at his son, who looked glum as he turned to gaze out the window.

Anna's face was pinched as she freed her hand, backing up until she was standing between the Stantons. Both Abe and Elijah glared at Blaze, who continued to avoid eye contact with all of us.

"What can we do for you, Terrence?" Abe's voice was terse and noticeably light on the hospitality.

The man seemed to be in no hurry, wiping his hands carefully on a satin handkerchief before depositing it into the trash, his nose crinkling in disgust as he did.

"Blaze thought you people could use some help. And of

course, when a son calls, a father comes," he replied, his tone glib.

You people? I took the man in, immediately despising his entitled sneer as he thoroughly perused the females in the room, his eyes lingering far too long on parts not appropriate for gawking at without a permission slip. There was some family resemblance—both men had a similar body structure and similarities around the nose and mouth—but it ended there.

Terrence Edwards' eyes were cold and black and sharp like a raven's. His face, despite the years he had on his son, was remarkably smooth and tight behind the deep tan, suggesting the finest surgical hands had sculpted his features into a younger, more vibrant model.

His slick hair had once been the color of his son's, now silvering at the hairline. His lips were full and what Leah called "plumpy"—another enhancement. If you had looked up the term "slimy" in the dictionary, his picture would have been the first entry. I wanted to punch him in his blinding veneers, which would probably turn out to be like tackling a shark.

The parallels were not lost on me and I decided to mind my manners.

It didn't mean I had to like it.

Something told me that my decision had made the mother who raised me proud. And for a moment, it was as though she had been sitting on my shoulder, reminding me that there are people in this world that we don't need to understand or embrace but that we must be aware of and accept that they too, serve a purpose. I sighed, even in death, my mother was making sure I behaved myself, no matter how extreme the circumstances.

Thank goodness for Leah, who had no such whisperings in her ear or any sort of filter as she trudged toward the man and thrust her hand out expectantly.

"Leah Campbell, friend of these guys."

She nodded at the group, her mouth forming an unattractive pucker when he clasped her hands with both of his and stared directly not at her eyes but at her assets, essentially giving her front side a once over, which ended at chest level. Hers.

"Mmmm…that would make you the famous AJ." His words oozed out like slime from a slug as his vile gaze left Leah and lasered in on yours truly.

"Arianna," I replied, staying firmly planted in place, crossing my arms to cover my front…parts. "Arianna Jackson." I didn't add that only friends were allowed to call me AJ.

He finally released Leah, both physically and optically. I was surprised his retinas were still intact. I didn't fault her for needing a quick reprieve to collect herself as she squatted to pet Nicoh, who somehow managed to find time for a nap in the middle of the commotion. She glanced up at me and had I not known better, would have thought she'd sucked on a lemon. I knew it wasn't Nicoh's desperate need for a bath that had her in a pucker and offered her a single head nod.

I, too, could use another shower after the man's vulgar raking.

Oblivious to his effects on the females in the room—though the males, including his son, appeared equally disgusted given the round of frowns—the elder Edwards looked around the office, rubbing his hands together.

"Not bad, Abe. You either, Elijah. You taking care of my little Anna here?"

I nearly gagged before Abe took a step toward the man. "Anna's quite capable of taking care of herself, Terrence, though I'm sure I don't need to tell you that."

Edwards seemed unaffected by the younger man's tone, so Abe prodded him along as he crossed his meaty arms. "What can we help you with?"

I took the translation to mean—so that we can get you to

move along as quickly as possible, preferably before I have to launch you out the window.

Personally, I would have paid to see that. Then again, he *was* Blaze's father. Show a bit of respect, AJ, I chanted silently to myself.

"Oh, no, no." Edwards wiggled a finger, at no one in particular.

He puffed up his chest and for a moment, I was hoping he hadn't confused us with one of his trial juries, having seen him on one of those cable television channels that streamed live court footage—chalk it up to a bad case of the flu—it was a week I would never get back and something I hoped to never witness again.

"I've come to help you. My sources tell me that my boy here has gotten himself into some trouble—another one of the pranks he typically finds himself entangled in. Only this time, I hear his friends are paying the price for his shenanigans." He paused to flick an invisible speck of lint from his sleeve. "Anyway, it's about time the entire lot enters the corporate world. Speaking of which, I can still get you a spot in the firm if you take the bar, old boy."

All of us glanced at Blaze in confusion, as we'd been unaware he'd even graduated college, much less gone to law school. Anna just looked out the window, shaking her head, knowing this was the direction the conversation would take if Edwards was called in.

I gave Blaze credit. He took his hands out of his pockets, squared his shoulders and looked his old man straight in the eyes.

"Thanks, Father, but, no. At least, not right now. I'm working on a project…one that could do some real good for the community and shed light on an important environmental issue. We could change the way—"

Edwards shook his head, cutting his son off. "It's not going to win you an Academy Award, much less a People's Choice Award, though, is it?" He paused but it seemed more for effect than to elicit commentary, as he promptly continued berating his son.

"People aren't interested in that frivolous, frou-frou stuff. If they're going to spend their hard-earned money, they want entertainment—action, superheroes, zombies. Not this artsy fartsy, I'm-sharing-a-message crap you and your beach bum doper crowd tend to favor."

"That's not exactly what I said, Father. You're not listening, as usual." Blaze fisted his hands at his side, his face reddening at his father's criticism. "Besides, what would you know about hard-earned money, anyway?"

The last part came out barely as a whisper though everyone with ears had heard each venom-filled, scathing word. If he wanted to scald the man, however, he probably should have notched up the burner, because the man appeared unaffected, bored and unapologetically uninterested.

In fact, Edwards didn't even bother to venture a glance at his son, instead checking his cell phone as though the entire outing was an inconvenience.

"That's quite enough of your incessant whining. You're certainly one to talk about hard work." Before Blaze could interject, the man waved his hand. "Never mind that, I'll get everything taken care of, before your mother hears about it from her gossipy friends. Woman doesn't need to worry about you any more than she already does. As it is, I'll have to send her to that spa in Helsinki once she hears about your latest buffoonery. It will cost me a damn fortune, I'll have you know."

Blaze rolled his eyes, shaking his head. Apparently, it was a familiar ploy his father used.

Fortunately, Elijah stepped in, adding a bit of reality to the man's drama-filled existence.

"Mr. Edwards. We're both lawyers. And while I don't

currently practice, nor would I be presumptuous enough to put myself in your shoes, I'd hate for you to make a judgment before having a clear understanding of the entire situation.

"Your son, his associates, as well as Anna and her friends have all been the targets of serious threats, made by an assailant for reasons unknown. Rather than take the situation on himself, your son had the foresight to employ the services of a very competent private investigator, on my recommendation. I believe you are familiar with her father, Max Decker," Elijah paused, letting the words sink in but Edwards continued to look bored as he tapped his foot and stared at his phone, probably scanning his social media feeds.

After a few moments, he looked up, those black eyes revealing nothing. "Are you trying to impress me, Stanton? Or perhaps, looking for more suitable employment? Either way, whatever's going on is nothing more than child's play. I'm simply here to clean up the mess."

Abe shook his head, rubbing his temples, as though the conversation had made him weary. "I don't think you understand my brother, Terrence. It's not that simple. It's gone beyond idle threats. And frankly, you're involvement could very well put you in the middle of an already dangerous situation."

When the man glanced up, there was a predatory interest in his eyes. "Oh, do tell," he replied, a cruel twitch at the corner of his mouth.

"It's progressed—" Abe started.

Edwards waved a hand. "I'm well aware of the motorcycle accident, Stanton. Yet another result of the recklessness of children."

Abe held Blaze back before he could advance on his father but Edwards had already caught the movement, as well as the venom in his son's eyes.

"Oh? Am I wrong?" Edwards mocked him, forming an "o"

with his mouth before sneering. "My sources suggested the investigators have yet to submit their report. Right now, it's deemed nothing more than an accident. Besides, until they have a body there's nothing concrete to go on." He sighed. "Poor Bryce. It will probably be ruled as an unfortunate accident. Or a suicide. He was a known drug user, after all."

"He was twelve and it was a little pot," Blaze replied through gritted teeth. "Those records should be sealed."

Edwards raised a hand. "Riiiight. Just like your other pals. Always someone else, isn't it, son?"

"Don't call me that, you bastard!" This time it took Abe, Elijah and Anna stepping in to restrain him as Edwards smirked at his son's outburst.

I looked at Leah and from the look on her face, I wasn't sure which of us wanted to punch him in the throat more. In the end, it was Elijah who verbally backhanded the snark out of him.

"Alright, Edwards, we'll play it your way. Apparently, the boys in your line of work don't consider cold-blooded murder to be cause for concern." He paused before adding, "Nah, that's more like a light snack for the people you tend to represent. When we identify and catch this guy, we'll be sure to pass along your number. It's more up your alley, anyway…choosing thugs over family." Elijah paused to tap his chin. "Wait…let me rephrase that —family who don't conform to your sick mold."

It wasn't a question and the man didn't seem overly offended, appearing more bored by the tongue-whipping as he tucked the phone into his breast pocket and picked at his manicured nails, pausing to look at his son, without really looking at him.

"Blaze, it's about time that you realize the family name is not one to be taken lightly. And in case you need to be drug by the nose to get the point I have been at pains to make—it's time to grow up. In the meantime, if memory serves, you beckoned me here and asked for my help. If it's going to happen, it will happen…on my terms."

"Then it appears I've been hasty in asking for your assistance," Blaze replied, gesturing toward the door before adding, "And for the record, everyone in this room warned me not to call you and it appears they were right. Thanks to you, I owe them my apologies for the dramatics they've just be forced to witness.

"Having said that, please feel free to leave, Father, and pretend you never heard any word about this matter that I—or your spies—have relayed. You're accustomed to it, so just maintain the status quo. Tell Mother you haven't heard from me and we'll just agree to be civil—or as civil as you are able to fake.

"Now, if you would excuse us, my friends and I have a murderer to catch. And, as a final parting request—don't let the d-o-g bite you in the butt on your way out. AJ tells me he's a bit feisty when he senses trouble in his midst."

I could have kissed Nicoh. He selected that very moment to sit upright, as though he'd been eavesdropping on the humans' conversation the entire time, showing Edwards a full set of fangs as he yawned, all while loudly releasing a noxious round of stink bombs.

Edwards frowned and backed away as my noble beast stood and shook off, advancing on the newcomer in our group. Before Edwards could protect his private parts—which the man hastily attempted to cover—Nicoh gave him a firm once-over of his own, which left a noticeable wet spot on the front of his silk slacks, causing him to back out of the room in haste.

"I expected more, son," Edwards spat. "Your mother and I… are highly disappointed."

"So am I," Blaze responded, pointing toward the door.

The elder Edwards turned on his highly polished heels, pausing just before he exited. "I guess it's for the best, especially now that the EPA has been alerted to a potential contamination situation at that beach. And once it's confirmed, all the birdies, fishies and whatnot will need to be relocated, and the beach itself will no longer need to be preserved so that little tootsies can be stuck in the sand or women wearing bikinis two sizes too small can lounge in the sun to burn their unmentionables—"

Leah cut him off before he continued his diatribe, gritting out every word. "Meaning that once they've all been cleared out, the developers will able to request a rezoning of the area so that they can proceed to build their monstrosities."

Edwards shrugged. "It's just business, darling." Before she could respond, he sneered at his son, adding, "Of course, that's bad news for you, Blaze. No more little movie. Alas, it was always destined to fail, but you can't say I didn't warn you."

Blaze stepped toward his father until they were inches apart. "It's not a *movie* Father. And just how did you come by this information, anyway?"

Edwards smirked, tapping his finger to his temple. "Because I represent one of the investors, who is prepared to file a claim against the city, the government and you, Blaze, for loss of profits that could have been gained by development that, until now, your project has managed to stall."

And with that bombshell, he winked and left us watching the backside of that ridiculously expensive suit.

I hated to ruin a good exit line—so I didn't.

CHAPTER TWENTY

It turns out no one else wanted to either, as an uncomfortable silence whipped through the air, which had suddenly become unbearably warm.

It was Anna who spoke first, frowning as she absorbed Blaze's hangdog expression. "When will you learn?" Her tone was more sad than angry as she bit a nail and paced. "Sometimes, I just don't get you."

"Old habits, I guess," he replied so quietly, she was forced to step closer. "Then again, my father's more like a bad rash than a habit, isn't he?"

Anna squinted at him from beneath her bangs, shaking her head before releasing a small chuckle. Blaze moved to his fiancé and embraced her firmly, while the rest of us looked away or shifted positions so that we were not overtly invading what should have been a private moment.

"Did you ever consider emancipation as a child, Blaze?" Leah blurted out. Blaze shook his head, laughing. "'Cause that man? He's…something else."

"Oh, he's something all right," Blaze responded, this time his tone turning serious. "Unfortunately, in my haste, I think I've opened a can of worms."

"I was thinking more a vat of leeches," my best friend replied, scrunching her nose the way she typically did when one of us had forgotten to take out the trash.

"Now that he's aware of the situation, he'll find a way to insert himself into it," Anna replied, pulling away from her fiancé so that she could resume pacing.

Elijah shrugged. "Not much we can do about it now. We need to proceed as planned and stay on track. When Edwards rears his pitchfork again, we'll just need to take it as it comes—in whatever form it comes."

The rest of us nodded as Blaze put his hands in his pockets. "Again, I'm sorry about all of this, guys."

"Your father would have shown up sooner or later," Abe replied.

"You're probably right. Though I'm sure he was thrilled to shove my nose in it," Blaze murmured.

I changed the subject—something had been bugging me before Edwards had interrupted our brainstorming session.

"I don't know Decker as well as the rest of you but I don't think she was being completely up front with us." I paused to collect my thoughts. "Let me rephrase that. I don't believe she was lying, but she was definitely holding something back. Something important. And perhaps she had just connected the dots herself but honestly, I'm worried she's going to take it…whatever *it* is…on by herself. I think she feels she let you down, Blaze. And this is her shot at making it right."

When I was met with silence, I realized I'd overstepped. Every one of these people had either known or known of Decker longer than I had or had worked with her side by side and I'd crossed the boundary, so I quickly added, "Err… this is just what my gut is telling me."

I tried to stop her but Leah stepped in. "AJ's gut is right. Or it typically is, unless she's got low blood sugar." She paused to tap her chin. "Of course, there was that time she ate the whole container of red licorice and couldn't—"

I shot her a look, which she caught before adding, "I digress. Truth be told, I thought Decker was holding back, too. I mean, come on, that laundry list of tasks? I think we should start eyeballing that because one of those 'tasks' contains the nugget that leads us to her truth. Something she needs us to run up the flagpole to confirm or deny."

"Or something she wants us to see," I added. "In case things go haywire."

Elijah clapped his brother on the back. "You ready to deputize these guys? Or should I?"

Considering we'd just accused another private investigator of being less than truthful, they seemed far less angry than I thought they would be. In fact, their smirks suggested something else. I realized that they were not only amused—they were impressed.

"You're not Marshalls," Leah replied while looking each from head to toe. Knowing her as I did, she was hoping Raylan Givens would walk through the door, sporting a Stetson. "Or even cops," she added, squinting.

Oh no, I thought as I smacked my forehead, she'd moved onto her Dirty Harry phase.

"I think I have a plastic star stashed in the back of my desk drawer," Elijah offered, chuckling.

"Guns would be better," she replied, "and a taser."

Both Anna and Blaze laughed at the Stanton's expressions. Elijah was dumbfounded, his mouth hanging open and Abe, well, he was just not having it.

"Honestly, I'd prefer you didn't have either, though a gun might be safer."

"Now we're getting somewhere." Leah was smug as she put a hand out. "I'm gonna need ammo, too, Stanton."

Abe crossed his arms, trying to keep from laughing, though the quirk at the corner of his mouth gave him away.

"I don't know. Can either of you shoot?"

"Can we shoot?" Leah waved a hand. "I've been going to the range with my boyfriend—who, I'm sure I don't need to remind you, is a highly skilled homicide detective. And AJ—well, you've heard of Action Jackson, right?"

"Mmm, yes, your notoriety precedes you both," Abe replied. "Forget I asked."

"Tease." Leah snorted and gave me a sideways glance.

I could offer her nothing more in return than a shrug.

"I think you are onto something, AJ," Abe said, putting the kibosh on the shenanigans and refocusing the conversation. "I think we probably all agree." He opened his hands and everyone —Elijah, Anne, Blaze, Leah and I—nodded. "But that the answer lies in the list of busywork she gave us? Pure genius, Campbell."

Leah gave a little bow while I blushed. I wasn't sure what caused me to pipe up. Something about Decker told me that despite our backgrounds, the two of us had more similarities than differences and in this situation she'd done exactly what I would have. Only, considering the gravity of the mistakes I'd made along the way, I feared she had used up her only lifeline and given us nothing more than an unraveling ball of string.

Anna nodded. "Yeah, I don't know her as well as these guys but she did seem a bit piecemeal with the info." She turned back to Leah and me. "At what point did you think she was going off the range?"

Leah waved a hand at me, indicating that now that I'd started the ball rolling, I needed to continue.

I paced, uncomfortable about having so many pairs of eyes trained on me. "Oh, I don't know. All of it seemed out of order…

possibly on purpose, but I think maybe my feelers went up when she started talking about Cam."

"You're thinking that she might have realized, after-the-fact, that's she'd actually seen it, too?" Elijah asked, rubbing his chin. "She was on the crew, after all." He looked at Blaze, who shrugged and nodded. "Okay, let's break it down."

Anna grabbed a dry erase marker, strode to the white board, surveying it before she wiped it clean, after which she wrote "Cam," drew a box around it and extended a few lines from that.

"Cam said people were blocking the shot at the beach that day and until he approached them, didn't think much of it. It was their reaction that piqued his interest, though at the time it wasn't obvious what they were up to or why they ran. And when he saw them on subsequent occasions, they weren't in his shot so he didn't bother with them, but was still curious about their presence."

She drew a line and another box with a couple of stick people and a question mark.

Elijah turned toward Blaze. "You mentioned that based upon the timing, that portion of the film had likely been destroyed in the storage unit fire."

Blaze nodded. "Everything we had—camera, film, lenses—everything filmed prior to that day was lost in the fire," Blaze replied. "It's all documented…for insurance purposes. The police also have a copy."

"So, what did you do after the fire?" I asked. "You had the tent but from what I could tell, that was temporary and something you packed up and took with at the end of each day," I paused and Blaze nodded, "so who was responsible for packing it up…and transporting it?"

"We all were," Blaze replied. "There was too much for any one vehicle and depending on who was shooting, that's who took care of everything for that day."

"And you just left it in your vehicles?" Leah asked, raising a brow.

Blaze shook his head. "We stored most of it at Bryce's. He was the only one with a garage and a way to secure it." He caught a few of our questioning looks and added, "He has some pretty sweet custom cabinetry that was built by the previous owner for his gun collection."

"So whatever you have now, meaning anything you weren't using the day of the accident—it's all at Bryce's?" I prodded.

"Yeah, Bryce actually dropped some stuff off the morning before…the accident." He looked out the window, frowning. "His wife hated the fact he stored our stuff there. She wanted him to rip it out and use the space to build a laundry room, you know, so that they didn't have to run all the laundry in the house. With all those kids, she got tired of having to listen to the washer and dryer running next to the master bedroom at all hours." Blaze released a long breath before continuing, "He was planning on building her that laundry room as an anniversary surprise. And now, he'll never have the chance."

Anna went to him and placed her hands on his shoulder. "We can help, Blaze. We can help Sasha and the kids get through… whatever. Together."

"I doubt she'll come back," he replied. "There's nothing left for her here and when they find Bryce, she'll take him home."

Elijah cleared his throat and shifted the conversation back. "Do you think that Bryce had something in his garage that he wasn't aware he had?"

Blaze turned toward the group and nodded. "Anything is possible but honestly, I don't know how anyone could figure him for a target. He had the biggest heart…Cam, too. So much life to live. How could either one of them have been targets…for this?" He looked at us, almost pleading for an answer that none of us had.

At least not yet.

Abe walked toward the other man and placed a hand on his shoulder. "I realize that, Blaze. Really, I do. And while we don't have answers, we'll get them. We're closing in." When Blaze frowned, he added, "Hear me out. AJ and Leah are onto something. Maybe Bryce had something he didn't know was important, which is why he ended up becoming a target. Maybe that's what got Cam killed, too.

"Something else I'm curious about—before the accidents, how were he and Bryce getting along? Did they have a good relationship?" When Blaze nodded, Abe continued, "When they weren't working, did they spend time together, you know, tossing back a few beers, shooting the crap? Winding down?"

Blaze shrugged. "Yeah, but Bryce had a family and Sasha would have pitched a fit if he tied one on too often, rather than spending time with her and the kids. She already rode him about working so much and didn't fully understand what he did all day.

"Don't get me wrong, Sasha's a nice gal but she's also demanding and used to being a daddy's girl, which is a sweet gig when he happens to be the CEO of a luxury car company. When Daddy threatened to cut her off if she married a bum like Bryce, she figured he was bluffing, called it and lost. To her credit, she stood by her decision and never looked back. And except for the fact I just learned about his financial problems, I thought he did a pretty damn good job of taking care of his family.

"And Cam, well, he had Destiny. Spent most of his time with her and even helped her out at the bar when he wasn't working on the film. Pretty much could have earned himself a second salary but he never asked her for anything, other than her attention— which for anyone who knows her—didn't come easy, no matter who you were or how hard you tried. It's just the way she's always been."

He looked away from Anna, who stared intently at him as he

so easily discussed Cam's girlfriend, who had once been his as well.

It was an awkward exchange and I couldn't help but feel the need to fill the void. "I've only recently met her and while she did seem a bit rough, I also got the sense she genuinely cared about Cam."

"She does. I can't imagine what this must be doing to her." Blaze stopped short, his eyes wide. "God, Destiny—with everything that's happened, I had totally forgotten about her. Do you think she knows…about Cam?"

"I'm sure she does." Anna rubbed his arm. "Police have likely made their way to her by now."

"Still, I…should…call her," he replied, looking at his fiancé. "Go."

Blaze excused himself but returned almost as quickly, his brows furrowed. "Huh, no answer on her cell and her voicemail is full. Called the bar and her head bartender hasn't seen her, nor did he seem aware of what had happened to Cam. I'm pretty sure he would have said something if he had. Anyway, wasn't sure it was my place, so I didn't fill him in." He looked around the group, his head bowed as though he was feeling a bit sheepish.

"I think that was probably for the best," Elijah responded as the rest of us nodded. "If Destiny is off dealing with things, then she needs her staff to focus on running the business. I'm sure she'll fill them in when the time is right, in her own way."

"Thanks for saying that, man," Blaze replied and the two fist-bumped. "Thanks, all of you." He gave us each a quick head nod.

Abe picked up where we'd previously left off. "Sorry to keeping rehashing this, but getting back to Cam and Bryce, surely there were conversations between the two of them that you weren't privy to, maybe about what was going on with the threats —perhaps Cam even mentioned what he'd seen at the beach?"

"Well, yeah sure. We weren't joined at the hip. I'm sure they did stuff together that I don't know about, just as I might have met either one of them for a burger, a morning surf, whatever."

"But as far as you know, they were getting along ok?" Abe prodded.

"Not sure where you are going with this but we all had our differences from time to time. We're all bullheaded but it's nothing that ever got out of hand. We've been around each other too long for that. There are egos but then there are brothers. And the lot of us were brothers," Blaze replied.

"I get that. So, let me ask you this—were these brothers bummed when you brought Decker on? I know you hired other crew but Decker didn't possess the same…skill set as the rest of you. There had to be some resentment."

Blaze squinted at Abe. "I'm still not sure what you're getting at."

Elijah piped in, though I doubted Abe needed his brother to speak for him. "We're just trying to figure out if there was a possibility that Decker's cover was blown before you told Bryce."

Blaze stepped toward Elijah, poking a finger at his chest, millimeters shy of making contact. "Are you saying that I'm to blame for involving Decker in the first place and that we put her in jeopardy by letting her go off on her own?"

Elijah raised a hand. "Chill, Blaze. There's no blame being assigned here. And as far as 'letting' Decker go?" He shook his head and released a harsh, clipped laugh. "No one tells Decker to do anything, much less asks if she can do it. No, it was her choice and she wasn't asking for permission. It's not in her vocabulary, nor in her job description."

It was as though the helium had been released from Blaze's balloon as he simultaneously stepped back and tossed both hands up in surrender. "I can't be responsible for tragedy—any more tragedy, that is."

"We're not asking you to, Blaze," Abe replied. "We're taking responsibility for whatever happens here on out. We may just need your…resources…when the time is right."

"And I don't think they mean your dad, either," Leah added, creating a few shocked looks followed by a round of snickers. "Sorry, guess that goes without saying with this crowd."

"At least she's handy for comic relief," I added, receiving a dirty look from my BFF. "Having said that, we need to keep our wits about us—we *are* on the same side, after all." I pointed at every person, until I received a head nod. "Okay then, let's get to it."

"I think this is a good time to start looking at Decker's list. No matter the reason, she wanted us to focus on three things," Anna replied, returning to the white board. "One, identify the status of Bryce's investigation; two, follow up with Frank and three, review the real estate troublemakers."

Abe pointed. "Blaze, Elijah and I can tackle the first two, make the necessary phone calls, which leaves the real estate list to you, Leah and AJ, if you think you can handle it?"

Anna opened her mouth but I beat her to the punchline. "You boys have your tasks," I replied, crossing my arms. "Do you need us to draw you a map in crayon? Or do you think *you* can handle it?"

"I think we've been dismissed," Blaze replied.

"Smart boy." Leah's stance mirrored mine, though we both knew we were just yanking their chains so that we could do what we did.

Get stuff done.

"Good training," Blaze murmured, glancing at his fiancé.

"Good answer," Anna retorted, pointing at the door. "Now go."

Once the boys left, Anna firmly shut the door behind them.

"Alright, Anna, what are you thinking?" Leah asked, settling onto the corner of the desk.

"Let's start with the primary developer," she replied.

"Okay, but don't we have to make an appointment or something?" I asked.

Anna shook her head. "We walk straight through the front door and politely ask to see the head honcho. If the admin gives us pushback, we'll inform her that we have the media on speed dial and we'll direct them to park their trucks on the front steps with the intent of exposing their interference in the beach preservation efforts. Or at least that's what we'll make them believe, until we get what we want."

I nodded.

The element of surprise.

And the threat of mischief.

I always knew I dug her style.

CHAPTER TWENTY-ONE

Decker

I disconnected, feeling a little guilty that'd I withheld some of the goods.

Then again, I needed to make amends. A lot of this was on me.

I'm not saying I was responsible for setting up the events that had transpired. But things had put me off my game—I'd bought a few lies along the way. And now, people were dead.

On my watch.

It's time to pay the piper, Decker. I could hear Pops mumbling to me from behind dentures that didn't quite fit.

Damn straight, Pops. I can make this right.

And so I'd lied to the people who were relying on me.

I accepted that.

And I moved on.

It had, in my opinion, been simply a lie of omission. The real lie I still needed to weed out. And I certainly didn't intend to involve these people any more than I already had.

It was, after all, a hunch and I had to be sure.

Once you weed the truth from the lies, you realize it's been there all along. Threads. Cracks. The stuff that makes for a good whodunit—until it pits you in the middle, along with the people who hired you to keep them and the ones they care about safe. And you failed them. Only you didn't. You were just off your game. You were too busy looking for the enemy sitting in the shadows when he was standing right in front of you from the start, bold as brass.

Before he died, Pops always said that if he'd paid more attention, he would've been able to close my mother's case and bring her murderer to justice. There were times I thought he was onto something but when the light went out in his eyes, I figured what little hope he had left had slipped away, along with the contents of whatever bottle he'd found himself at the bottom of.

I suppose I should have thanked Destiny for calling me that first time, having recognized my old man from the media. The conversation had been short and she'd been understanding. She'd lost both parents to the same devil.

From that point on, she always met me out front of the bar, where Pops would either be on his knees puking his guts out on the pavement or slumped on her front bench, his cap in his hand. I'd pay his bill, adding in a sizable tip for whatever obstinate, boisterous behavior she and her staff had to endure during the course of his visit.

Truth be told, I preferred not having to enter Destiny's establishment to retrieve him, not because I was embarrassed by my Pop's antics.

It was the picture she had of him on her wall.

I'd seen it on my first visit and hadn't cared to see him immortalized in this manner, with his cheeks flushed with drink as some Barbie raised her top and pressed her ampleness into his face. At that moment, a mass of emotions washed over me— anger, pain, regret—the same ones I knew my father felt as he drowned himself in his bottle of woe as he realized my mother would never come back, regardless whether her murderer was caught.

Sometimes I'd wished I had told him that there was never going to be a happy fairy tale ending. Unlike my father, who held onto the fantasy, I realized the moment my mother was ripped from our lives that there would be no justice—because I knew who had killed her.

People may wonder why I hadn't run to my father, screamed at the top of my lungs and pointed that finger he wanted me to point. It hadn't occurred to my child brain—all I wanted was to keep myself and my Pops safe.

It wasn't until years later that I started remembering things that had been hidden in that child brain. At first, I wondered if they had been influenced by my dad's rantings, as he pulled out the gruesome files of my mother's death pose and forced me to sit and listen as he reviewed every last detail surrounding the last moments of her life, which ended when she was slaughtered like an animal.

Over time, the images hazily flooded in, in no particular order until one day, they played like scenes from a movie. I realized I had seen my mother's murderer as I hid, heard him speak, his voice haughty as he cut her from throat to pelvis, extracting the child that he claimed he had fathered.

As she bled, he chastised her, saying that no bastard should have to live to face the cruelties of the world in the way he had been conceived. The fear in my mother's eyes told me that if it were true, she had not been a willing participant.

He had gone on to rant about his own family and how they would suffer as a result of whatever it was my mother had done to venture into his line-of-sight. Considering she was both a wife and mother who worked two jobs—one at a law office in the morning, copying papers and running errands for the legal secretaries; the other at a local video store at weekends—and was going to school part-time so that she could gain employment as a court reporter, I couldn't imagine when she would have had time to "venture into his line-of-sight" but somehow, they had crossed paths.

Years later, I would learn she'd kept the rape quiet for my father's sake, which may have been her downfall, if not my father's and mine.

It was only when I came face-to-face with the man at my father's funeral—the devil who had violated and murdered my mother, ripping his unborn child from her womb—that I realized the answer had been standing in front of Pops all along. And while the man may not have been aware that I had seen him all those years ago, I saw him now.

Problem was, while I had witnessed his crimes, the only proof I had were memories extracted from a child's brain. And until I could figure another way to get him and put my mother and father to rest, side by side, in both body and spirit, I had to focus on the thing that drove me and made me whole—which meant following in Pop's footsteps.

And, like him, I hadn't listened to my own advice—the answer had been right in front of me all along.

Only this time, I wasn't sure which devil was worse, the one who'd murdered my mother and allowed my father to die inside. Or the one who stood out in the open—brazen, indifferent, compassionless—who took what he wanted no matter the cost and tossed it into the faces of those he'd inflicted heartbreak and pain. In the end, they were no different. And now, I would take one down, so that I could go after the other.

I pulled into the driveway, walked straight into the garage and smiled—the missing piece of the puzzle had been there the entire time.

I reached for the camera, in perfect condition—despite being declared as one of many losses of the storage unit fire—smiling as I watched the footage.

Oh yes, I had been there that day—and there it was, in the background. Not in the shadows but out in the light of day. And suddenly, everything made sense.

I should have been surprised by the visitor who caught me from behind but wasn't. My response was one of disappointment as I slowly turned and looked death in the eye, grinning as the hammer was pulled and a snarling hiss of lead bit my flesh before my world went black.

Sorry Pops, guess we both learned our lessons the hard way.

Only this time, I made sure the truth would be revealed and justice would be the victor.

For once, evil wouldn't be slipping casually into the shadows. I was giving it a one-way ticket to hell.

CHAPTER TWENTY-TWO

I bit my lip to prevent a snark from slipping out when the slim brunette in a low-cut crimson double-breasted power suit tersely directed us to cool our jets after the Renegade Three, a title I had privately bestowed upon us—that would have been four had we not left Nicoh behind to hold down the fort at Stanton Investigations—descended upon the real estate developer's office, which had too many names for my sleep-addled brain to process.

We'd been deposited into a conference room off the main reception area as she fetched the CEO, because I was sure Power Suit didn't want us mingling or sharing hair tips with their clientele in the waiting room. It turned out to be fortuitous, as the conference room also housed scaled models of the firm's current projects.

Each had its own set of carefully positioned spotlights, poised on platforms that rotated to the rhythm of a symphony echoing through speakers that were embedded into the walls and carefully hidden from view. Also present were several cameras, only they were visibly perched in every nook and cranny, perhaps to serve as a warning to any visitor who was tempted to pluck an apple from the toy-sized trees displayed in a few of the models, designated for ventures planned in Washington State.

"When was the last time you saw an apple orchard lining a golf course?" Leah pointed and we all snickered.

"About as many times as I've actually been on a golf course," I replied. "Miniature golf is more my speed."

Anna chuckled. "I'll keep that in mind when I'm planning pre-wedding activities. It'll be right up there with the sumo suit smackdown."

We continued to wander in silence from one model to the next. I was a little overwhelmed by the sheer volume of proposed shopping communities, luxury homes, entertainment complexes, sports arenas and on and on. The developer had created something for every vision that would easily whet any investor's appetite. It was like walking through an amusement park and having an endless supply of tokens.

It was Leah who spotted it first—a model that depicted a luxury beach community outside L.A. along the PCH that included almost anything you could dream of, from ginormous mansions to condos with a penthouse option—complete with rooftop pools; summer rentals, all with butler and maid services— to high-end shopping. There were also personal concierges assigned to handle any minor convenience, as well as any type of transportation available, whether residents choose to tootle about the neighborhood and shops, run up and down the beach or hit the waves.

And of course, you couldn't have a community without entertainment. There were both movie and stage theaters with private seating, high-end bowling alleys and pool halls that really were more social clubs, art galleries, gelato shops, candy shops, juice shops, dance clubs, cigar and smoke clubs, oxygen bars and of course, establishments catering to adults—including wine bars and craft breweries. Of particular interest was the beach-themed sports bar.

"Wonder if Destiny would find this amusing?" Leah pointed at the tiny surfboards that served as the establishment's doors.

We peered inside and like every other space in this massive model, the little bar had been crafted with the same meticulous detail and was outfitted with the same items one might see in a full-scale model—pool tables, dart boards, a makeshift dance floor with a stage for a band. There were even patrons seated at the bar being served by a buxom barkeep who was position behind.

"I doubt it," Anna murmured, peering at the exquisite detail of each structure.

"It's just massive. I didn't realize the beach was this large." Leah hunched down so she could peer in the windows of the various buildings, poking her finger inside one of the penthouses to get a better look inside the closet, which was filled top to bottom with goodies. "It kind of makes you feel like a voyeur, doesn't it?"

I backed away, having just noticed two figures smooching in the corner of the beach bar. "The people won't mind, Leah—you do realize they are not real?"

Leah shook her head before breaking into a round of snorts that were so loud I was convinced Power Suit would descend upon us.

"That's exactly my point, chickadees. Look at the square footage they've noted on this plaque. My math skills aren't great but I believe it translates to several dozen miles. So, if I've counted all my fingers and toes correctly, they are gonna need more than the span of that little beach where Blaze was filming to build this."

"She's right," I commented. "In order to fit all of this, they'd not only need the beach front and the length of that town, they'd need at least two or three of the beach communities on either side."

Anna put a hand to her mouth. "They weren't just going to build a luxury community inside an existing town, they were going to consume communities like it, forcing the current residents out so that they could erect their monstrosity."

"And permanently rid themselves of any external issues," I replied.

"Meaning any land the Environmental Protection Agency or others could prevent from been zoned for building," Leah added.

Anna started to say something but her phone vibrated. "What's up, Abe?" She put the phone into speaker mode—low enough that it would not alert Power Suit—and set it in front of the sports bar. It made for an odd doorstop.

"For starters, we talked to the guys working on Bryce's bike. They've taken it apart, put it back together, recreated the accident, both in a simulation and in the field using a similar bike and everything consistent with sabotage. Even if Bryce hit the brakes, they wouldn't have engaged—which accounts for the lack of tire marks—and as far as the loosened lug nuts, it wasn't due to normal wear and tear or lack of maintenance. They were tampered with as well, though whatever was used didn't leave markings on the metal."

"Don't mean to sound snarky, Stanton, but that confirms what we already suspected. Am I missing something?" Leah snapped.

"Wasn't quite finished there, Campbell, but I'll let you apologize later, in private," Abe replied. "For now, we can just chalk it up to those reporter idiosyncrasies of yours."

My best friend fisted her hands, though she did a good job of biting her tongue, given her sour expression.

"Anyway, while this news may not be the icing on the cake, it does confirm sabotage. It also adds another element of intrigue." When he paused, Leah gave the phone a 'let's hurry it along' gesture and as though sensing her impatience, Abe continued, "After examining the various bike parts, they started cleaning it up, separating out the oil, grime, debris, dirt and other materials from the blood. And while blood was present, there wasn't enough. And what was there appeared to be old, maybe from an ankle cut or gash."

"Okay, maybe Bryce was tossed free when he went over and while the bike got caught up, he continued down the cliff into the ocean, where he was swept away. If he had gotten caught on the bike, it would have held him in place, prevented him from falling…" Anna's voice trailed off.

"Or crushed him," Abe replied. "Either way, the sabotage had one clear intention. Bryce had to die."

"But without a body, his wife, his children, his friends have no closure." This time Anna sounded bitter, her face pinched in pain as she batted at the corner of her eye.

"I doubt the person who did this cared one way or the other, as long as the job was done and he got his message across," Abe replied, quickly adding, "Sorry, didn't mean to come off as insensitive, Anna, it's just been a long day, for all of us."

She nodded at the phone, despite the fact he could not see her. "I understand. Anything else?"

Abe let out a long breath. "Well, Frank said the bomb was pretty rudimentary, even found a video online outlining how to make one in almost exactly the same manner."

"So we're not dealing with a pro," Leah confirmed, biting a nail.

"Well, you're not dead are you?" Abe's comment was met with silence.

I didn't dare venture a glance at my two friends. I was guessing it wasn't appreciated, considering we'd been on the receiving end of the threat, while he'd been safely in his sports car on the way back from Vegas.

As if sensing his misstep, which to be honest, was unlike him, Abe added, "Sorry, can't seem to keep my foot out of it today. Let me rephrase. A professional bombmaker, no, but definitely a motivated individual who has a varied skill set. He's tampered with a motorcycle, rigged a bomb, started a fire and was able to pull off a variety of other incidents. He also holds no bones about cold-blooded murder or getting up close and personal to deliver it. This is one cold monster we're dealing with."

"Smartest thing you've said all day." Leah placed her hands on her hips, enunciating each word as she stood inches from the phone.

Abe ignored her and continued, "Blaze attempted to follow up with Destiny again, got nothing."

"She wasn't able to give him anything?" Anna asked.

"Nope. He still couldn't reach her. Even tried the bartender again, who still hadn't seen her."

"Seems kinda odd to me," Leah replied. "She seems like the type to at least check in with her staff."

"People grieve in different ways, I guess."

He sighed, sounding even more tired than he had just moments before. "We also tried Decker earlier but like Destiny, it went to voicemail." There was an awkward pause and we heard movement. "Oh, crap, I just realized I got a voicemail when I was on the phone with Frank. Just a sec…" There was a beep as he put us on hold.

"You ever hear your boss sound so tired or act so out of sorts?" Leah asked, while looking at Anna.

"Ask me in about a month when *I'm* not so tired and out of sorts," she replied, rubbing her eyes.

Leah nodded just as Abe came back on, his voice choppy, like he was running. "I think we've got trouble. It was Decker. Didn't seem quite herself when she left the message…sounded short of breath and oddly cryptic, even for her." I heard a car door slam.

"Abe? You there?" Anna called to him, grabbing her phone. "Talk to me!"

"Sorry, just got back to the car. The thing is, Decker didn't really say anything…or anything that made sense, anyway."

Leah threw her hands up and gritted her teeth. "Use your words, Stanton. Where was she and what did she say, whether it made grammatical sense or not?"

"Elijah's got a friend—owes him a favor—tracking her cell. Will text us when he's got something."

"In the meantime, what do you think she was trying to say?" I repeated Leah's request, barely able to contain my own anxiety as I tugged on my ponytail.

At this rate, I'd be bald within the hour.

"That's the thing…something about the devil or evil or something being in front of you," he mumbled. "Hold on will ya? Elijah's got something." He didn't wait for a response and when he returned his voice had turned frantic. "Oh crap." We all huddled around the phone, waiting until he added, "She's at Bryce's."

CHAPTER TWENTY-THREE

I clipped my thigh on the corner of the model as Anna grabbed her phone and she and Leah started to run. I paused to rub the knot, noting that beach community and its residents kept moving and the occupants of the bar continued imbibing in their adult refreshment. For a split second, I considered joining them.

None of us made explanations to Power Suit as we burst from the conference room, surprising both her and a few of the clients waiting as we sprinted out the front door.

Leah couldn't help herself as she shouted to them over her shoulder, "It's a farce—escape while you can!"

It felt like it took hours to get from downtown to Bryce's empty house, though we managed to arrive ahead of the Stanton brothers. Despite the fact they had insisted we wait until they had an opportunity to assess the situation, Anna overrode their authority and gave us the thumbs-up to ignore them—stating it was just a recommendation and not an order.

She did, however, insist upon taking the lead and considering she was both a black belt and had the only weapon, we were happy to defer to her judgment and authority. The only problem was, there are some things for which you are never prepared for. Even the best-laid plans go awry.

As we approached Blaze's home, Anna released a small cry. I followed her gaze to the garage door, which by all accounts, should have been stuck in the open position. Protruding from beneath the door was an arm, lying in blood that had seeped from the other side. Though I recognized the hand, with its short black nails, it was the tattoo on the inside of the forearm that confirmed the identity.

Aequitas.

Justice.

Shoving the shock and horror aside, I ran to the garage door and searched for a way lift it. Anna found a small window on the side of the garage and after smashing it with the base of her gun, wove her fingers together with mine, creating a step to launch Leah through the opening. After a few crashes, followed by a series of obscenities, she pushed the garage's side door open and let us in.

The three of us knelt beside Decker and as Anna checked for a pulse, I pulled her arm free and clasped her hand, sucking in a breath when I found it was still warm but Anna shook her head. I shuddered, withholding a sob as I registered the fact that in her final moments, someone had caught Decker by surprise when they shoved a gun into her back and pulled the trigger. Even in death, Decker looked angry.

Though I was probably destroying evidence, I continued holding her hand and closed her eyes with the other as I allowed the tears that had been threatening to run free, not because I'd known Decker all that well but because I believed that we might have become friends. At the very least we would have been kindred spirits, as we'd both lost ones we loved to violence. Only my story had an ending, as dismal as it had been. Hers had not.

Both she and her father had gone to the grave searching for justice.

I bowed my head, as the irony of her choice of tattoos was not lost on me.

I spoke and even as I did, my voice sounded hollow and foreign. "She didn't deserve this." When no one responded, I added, "I'm gonna look around."

Deep down, I knew it was a ruse, a means to temporarily escape the situation. Of course, reality came rushing back and smacked me in the face as I grasped Decker's fingers for the last time, noting the warmth had only been supplied by my own. As I rose, I didn't bother wiping her blood off.

It should have disturbed me, but it didn't. It made me angry.

"Wait, AJ," Anna called after me, her voice quiet and without an ounce of conviction. "Abe and Elijah will be here soon. The police will come…"

I couldn't comprehend what I couldn't hear so I ignored them and walked out of the garage, hoping for a gust of fresh air that did not come. Neither of them followed and I doubted if they would but it didn't matter—I had other things on my mind.

Out of context, they made no sense.

Decker's cryptic voicemail.

The beach bar with the little surfboard doors in the developer's model.

The comment Destiny had made to Decker about her line of work.

I flashed to the picture in the Destiny's bar—the one of Decker's father.

If she'd known Decker before, then she'd known who—and what—she was all along.

Why hadn't she told Cam? Or any of her other pals?

Maybe she had.

Suddenly, the puzzle pieces snapped together and the bar in the model made sense.

And so did Decker's last message.

Even in her final moments, she had struggled to make sure her death hadn't been for nothing.

"Destiny," I murmured.

A familiar laugh erupted over my shoulder, causing me to spin on my heel. There she stood, leaning casually against the gate, arms crossed, as though she'd been waiting for me to venture out all night. Her multi-colored locks swayed in the breeze as her ample bosom threatened the boundaries of her fitted tank. The only other thing tighter was the pair of leather pants she wore, tucked into knee-high boots.

"I knew you were the smart one in the bunch."

I shrugged. "Not smart enough, as it turns out. Too late to save Decker."

"Decker and I had an old score to settle."

"One that involves shooting her in the back?" Destiny sneered, surveying me as I added, "Why did you do it?"

"Like I said…old score."

"Let me rephrase my question, then, and fast-forward to the current situation. Why did you set it all in motion?" I snapped, stepping toward the wild-haired monster. "Cam…Bryce…were their lives really worth the promise of moving your dumpy little bar into that fancy new development?"

"You're a cheeky one, aren't you?" she replied, still not moving. "And don't think for a moment that I don't know what you're doing."

"What am I doing?" I asked, leaning wearily against the garage. "I thought we were just two chicks having a little chat."

"Distracting me long enough so that your friends come out, guns blazing."

I put my hands up. "Ooh, you got me on that one, Destiny."

She snorted. "I might actually have grown fond of you, AJ. You've got balls. That's for sure. But right now, you're a means to an end—a way to ensure I get out of here." Her smile wouldn't have won her a place in a beauty pageant, though had there been any bloody meat lying around, I could have seen her gnashing at it, letting the juices run down her chin.

"I could just turn around and walk back into the garage, grab my friends and together we'll kick your butt. Or maybe I'll just let Anna shoot you." I thumbed over my shoulder. "Either way I don't care. Or…hey, why don't I just yell, let them know the psycho who terrorized Blaze's crew and murdered his friends stopped by for a little girl talk?"

"You could. But if you move from that spot, I'll press this little button here." She dangled what looked like a car remote from her index finger. "And boom. Your friends meet their maker. Same goes for you, if you call out to warn them."

"What about the Stantons?" I asked. "Surely you realize they're on their way?"

"Oh, I don't think they'll be coming…to your rescue, anyway." She laughed at my confused expression.

Truth be told, it wasn't one of my best looks.

"You see, I gave them a little shoutout, apologized for missing their calls and told them that I ran into the three of you and together, with Decker, we were heading to the beach to check out a lead."

I shook my head. "But they already know we're here."

"Do they, now?" She tossed her head back and released a maniacal laugh. "Come on, I think it's time we take a little bike ride."

"Well, darn, I don't have a helmet." I waved my hands and pretended to look around.

Destiny snickered. "Oh, I'm sure I can manage. I'll even let you wear mine."

"Gee, I couldn't have your brain matter on my conscience, if we crashed, that is," I replied, keeping my tone light as I took a small step back, hoping she wouldn't notice.

This time, she was less than amused as she advanced on me and grabbed my arm.

"I insist, AJ. And don't forget, keep it down." Destiny smirked, wiggling the remote in my face as she shoved me down the driveway.

I noted that both the hedges and Anna's vehicle blocked us from view.

"Can I ask you a question?"

"Depends."

"What was the deal with the video, anyway? Did it even exist?"

"It *did*." She snorted in my ear as we reached the opposite side street, where she'd parked her motorcycle behind another row of hedges.

"And? What was on it?" I prodded.

"Get on the bike, AJ." Destiny glared at me.

"You didn't say please," I replied crossing my arms. "And I don't think I will until you answer my question."

"Have it your way." Without looking back, Destiny raised the remote and pressed the button.

Over her shoulder, I watched as Bryce's garage exploded and burst into flames. As I opened my mouth to scream she cold-cocked me.

The last thing I remembered was her catching me, her breath hot on my ear as she whispered, "Like I said, AJ, have it your way."

CHAPTER TWENTY-FOUR

I awoke, my jaw throbbing, head foggy and butt sore as we bounced along the road. My arms were wrapped around her waist and secured at the wrists.

"Hang on!" Destiny yelled.

My head felt like it was in a cocoon. Somehow, after knocking me senseless, she had managed to get a helmet on my head. Thankfully, she had lowered the mask, which prevented the wind and the ends of her hair, now tied in a knot at the base, from snapping me in the face.

Though it made me nauseous to do so, I rose ever so slightly so that I could peer over her shoulder as we whipped around the curves of the open road. I immediately noted it was one I had traveled recently. In fact, we were heading in the direction of the beach where Destiny had told the Stantons to meet us. Had she been lying about making contact? Or was she going there to finish the job?

Suddenly, I remembered the explosion and started wiggling in an attempt to free myself.

"Stop that, or I'll unlatch these bindings and set you free," was the terse response.

"Do whatever you want, Destiny," I screamed at the back of her head. "You killed my friends, you evil—"

"As you wish," she yelled back, loosening one of the notches on my bindings before she jerked the bike and I came precariously close to falling off, until I managed to get a hold of her riding jacket and pull myself upright.

She tossed her head back and laughed—a wicked, dry sound. "I didn't think so." I clamped my mouth shut, releasing my grip ever so slightly. "Just hang on, this will be over soon."

"How does this end, Destiny?" I yelled at her back.

"I walk off into the sunset, AJ."

"Doesn't sound like much of a thrill," I retorted. "I hope it was worth it. Being broke and alone, that is."

"Why in the world would you think I'd settle for either?" she replied. "Maybe you're not so smart after all. No, AJ, I got exactly what I wanted. And more."

Before I could ask, I saw her glance in her rearview mirror and curse.

I attempted to look over my shoulder but my helmet blocked my view. I repositioned to give it another go just as Destiny leaned into the curve and accelerated. This time, I was the one tossing expletives out as the pavement whizzed past, just inches from my knee.

"Hold on, AJ, this is going to get hairy," she yelled, before releasing a whoop of excitement.

She zipped into the oncoming lane, passing not one, not two, but three vehicles before dodging back, narrowly missing a massive motor home. I didn't see the driver's eyes but if they were anything like mine, calling them saucers didn't do them justice.

Destiny laughed, reaching back to release her hair from the knot, allowing it to whip in the air and thwack me in the helmet before gripping the throttle. As we evened out on a straighter stretch, another motorcycle pulled alongside us. I squinted at the lifted mask and saw Blaze looking back. Once he'd caught my eye, he winked briefly before popping it down a gear and accelerating past Destiny's bike.

"Not this time, Blaze," Destiny screeched at his back as he moved in front of us. She gunned the bike, surging us forward until she could get in a position to clip his backside. As if sensing her maneuver, he dodged left, forcing us to the right, and precariously close to the narrow shoulder that separated us from plunging down the cliffs.

The lane was too narrow to ride in tandem but Blaze looked at Destiny, then at me. Then at my hands, still secured around Destiny's waist. Catching his expression, Destiny let out a shriek of laughter.

"You want her?" she snapped. "Go get her."

After releasing me from my bindings, she tilted the bike and attempted to dump me off, using her weight to finish the deed. My eyes widened as I fought to stay on the seat and Blaze, who witnessed the exchange, struggled to keep his bike in the lane as we careened from side to side.

Finally, Destiny worked me free and with her left arm, shoved me off. I bounced off the pavement and slid several hundred feet on the shoulder of the road. As Blaze shifted to avoid hitting me, the front of his bike collided with Destiny's and both toppled as they skidded toward the cliff side. Blaze managed to detangle himself from his bike but clipped the guardrail with his leg, bending it the wrong way as the remainder of his body slammed into me.

Destiny attempted to break away from her own bike but caught her boot on something as the bike careened over the edge. Without thinking, both Blaze and I grabbed for her but the bike's momentum pulled Destiny over, with Blaze and I close behind. Finally, her boot broke away and the bike continued down the cliff, crashing and bounding off the rock until it joined the water. Destiny was caught up in some brush, and though I had her wrist and Blaze had the back of her jacket, we were rapidly losing our hold on her.

"Let go," Destiny screamed. "Just let me go!"

"Not until you tell us why," Blaze bellowed.

"I don't owe you crap, Blaze, you remember that." Destiny struggled and broke free from his grip.

After overcoming his surprise Blaze latched onto me, as I still had Destiny's wrist but I too, was fighting fatigue.

"I got you, AJ, just hang on," he shouted. "Can you reach her with the other hand?"

I nodded. "Destiny, can you reach up, grab my arm?"

"I can." She met my eyes. "But I won't."

"Don't be like that. We're all gonna end up going over. Do you really want to go down like this?"

She chuckled at my poor choice of phrasing. "You crack me up, Arianna Jackson. Like I said before, you're a smart one— you've nearly got this thing figured out. Now go get the rest." She looked me straight in the eyes, shaking her head when she knew she had my attention.

"So no, you're not gonna die today. But I am."

And with that, Diamond Destiny released my hand and fell backward. I opened my mouth to scream but nothing came out as I watched her watching me, until her body collided with the rocks below and her vibrant hair covered her face. Even as her blood spilled into the water, I swore her eyes were still fixed on me.

Forever watching.

CHAPTER TWENTY-FIVE

I barely remembered Blaze pulling me into his arms once the floodgates broke. At that point, all I could see was the image of Destiny's eye's trained on mine as she fell away. I might have been mistaken, but I could have sworn she winked.

I did, however, remember the moment he finally took me by the shoulders, as injured as we both were, and shook me until I stopped apologizing, expressing his confusion.

My lips quivered as I tried to form the words that I hadn't wanted to release. Once I did, it meant they were true. And I couldn't allow it to be.

Decker was gone, and that was on Destiny.

But Anna, the love of his life, and my dear friend, Leah—those were both on me.

Oh sure, Destiny had rigged the garage and pushed the button but I had failed to stop her. Now she, too, was dead and though I wasn't all that torn up about it, she had essentially gotten away with murder.

Again.

And with her went the answers I needed.

Finally, I managed to blurt out, "Because they're all dead, Blaze. And it's my fault."

Of course, I started wailing again and the apologies continued until Blaze—despite his fractured leg and who knows what else—resorted to sitting on me in order to get me to calm down.

"Leah and Anna are fine, AJ," he whispered into my ear. His breath was hot and ragged. "They pulled Decker free and got out before Destiny blew the place to hell."

"But how?" I replied, noting it came out sounding more like a whimper than actual words.

"Let's just say, you aren't particularly quiet," Blaze replied, his tone mildly amused.

We both winced in pain as he shifted off of me and I sucked in a breath before responding.

"Are you sure?" My voice crackled as I wiped away yet another tear.

Blaze nodded, grimacing as he did so. I tried hard not to mimic his response but considering the way his leg was bent, it was a chore.

"Scout's honor. Elijah confirmed it."

I swallowed, peering at him as he shifted, barely managing an "okay."

He raised his head and studied me. "Are you…okay?"

"No." I hung my head, letting the hair that escaped from my ponytail to fall into my eyes.

Blaze nodded but frowned as he stared at the cliff, only inches away. Neither of us wanted to look. We didn't need confirmation.

I suddenly noted how eerily quiet it was. That would all change soon, so I mustered up the nerve to continue.

"Destiny said she called and redirected all of you to the beach." When Blaze nodded, I added, "Sounds like she was pretty convincing."

"Yeah, she can be…was. Whatever. Anyway, when we realized something was up—she was acting pretty cagey, even for Destiny—we decided to split up. Abe went to the beach, or at least started heading that way. Elijah and I each drove separately and had just gotten into the neighborhood when we saw Destiny peeling down the street with you on the back of her bike, so I broke off and followed while Elijah proceeded to the house. You seemed pretty out of it. Unconscious?"

I nodded and could feel my cheeks turning red. "She cold-cocked me. Still hurts like hell." I rubbed at the spot, quickly pulling my hand away when it only made the throbbing worse.

Blaze offered me a sympathetic nod. "You shouldn't feel bad. Destiny's thrown down on me on a few occasions." He tenderly raised his riding jacket and sweat-soaked t-shirt, exposing a two-inch section of pink scar tissue. "See this? Landed on a scuba spear when she fought me for control of a jet ski. Of course, at the time, we hadn't been in a battle to the death. Even then, I don't recall her feeling all that broken up about it. She'd considered it a victory, having gotten it away from me."

I winced. "Wow. Glad I never had the chance to get her to know her better." I quickly clamped my mouth shut, stumbling as I changed the subject. "Um, if you came after me, how do you know that Anna and Leah are…okay?"

I belatedly realized that if he hadn't already known otherwise, he wouldn't have been as calm as he was. And he certainly wouldn't be sitting here jabbering with the likes of me.

Understanding my confusion, he pulled an earbud out.

"This…is how I know. Of course, I lost my phone when I crashed but I'm sure the cavalry is coming. Abe's on his way back so he'll reach us first and should be able to offer assistance, but I would like to see my fiancé with my own eyes—make sure she's okay—I'm sure you'd like to do the same with Leah."

I nodded, imagining she was as worried about me as I was about her. Though I was overwhelmed, having gone from thinking that she and Anna had been blown to bits in Bryce's garage to learning they'd escaped relatively unharmed, I wanted to see it for myself.

"They'll probably need to stay put until the situation at Bryce's is under control and Decker is properly taken care of. I'm also sure law enforcement will be around to take statements here, too. After that, they'll probably want to take us both directly to the hospital to be checked out."

Blaze waved a hand. "We'll see about that. If we get lucky, maybe I'll know someone on the crew who will allow us to deal with it later."

I grimaced, realizing if I was hurting as bad I was, he must have been in an excruciating amount of pain.

"How is it?" I asked, nodding at his leg.

He puffed his lips and blew out a long breath before patting the injured limb.

"It'll be okay, once I get it set, again." He chuckled when my mouth dropped open. "Yup, I've broken it twice before—I'm just glad it wasn't this one." He nodded at the right leg, his riding pants torn at the knee. "I already have a few dozen pieces of metal pinning it together, so I'm not sure there's room for much more."

I shook my head, fascinated by the ease with which he dealt with his numerous injuries. "So you're kind of like a terminator or the Six Million Dollar Man."

He threw his head back and laughed. "I wish."

I guess if that had been true, he probably would have ridden right off the cliff, alongside Destiny and would have made sure she was dead. That would have made for an interesting ending, though it wouldn't have changed the outcome.

I looked toward the drop-off that we'd nearly plunged over and shuddered. "You handled the crash pretty well. You didn't fight the slide once you were off the bike—that was some quick thinking, Blaze."

"Meh, lots of practice." He shrugged. "Crashing, that is."

We both chuckled. I turned when I noticed him looking over my shoulder. "Here comes the cavalry. Or at least part of it."

The Ferrari slowed, stopping at a safe distance before Abe jumped out and jogged to us. "Got here as soon as I could—you two okay?" He squatted, giving us both a once over.

"Geez, AJ, you think you could manage to stay out of trouble just one time were all together?" I shrugged. "Both Anna and Leah are out of their minds with worry. Leah lost it when she saw Destiny haul you off. Anna wasn't in much better shape, which only made it worse when Elijah told her that Blaze took off after the two of you. Where is she, anyway?"

He stood, picked up a fender from Destiny's bike, then strode to the edge of the cliff and looked down, squinting before he tossed it over the edge.

I winced. "Um, Abe…evidence?"

"There's all the evidence they'll need," he grumbled, nodding at the wreckage, before turning his back and returning to us. "Better than she deserved, for what she did to Decker. And the rest." He looked away. "I hope she lived for a while and that it was painful."

I looked down. I couldn't bear to tell him that her death had been quick and that at the end, she had been…amused.

"I'd better give Elijah an update on you two. By the way, help should be on the way soon…I hope you're ready?" Blaze and I shrugged, like we had a choice in the matter.

After a brief conversation with his brother, he hung up and chuckled. "Despite being a bit banged up and more than a little pissy, Anna and Leah are fine. Leah had words with one of the EMTs when he told her that her hair had been singed. As it turned out, it was just her hairstyle. Guy won't be hearing the end of that. Both want to get to you and Blaze but they're not leaving until they're sure Decker is properly taken care of." Abe's squinted as his tone became serious. "I still can't believe she's gone."

Blaze looked away but not before I saw wetness fill his eyes.

I squeezed his hand. "It was her job, Blaze. There would have always been risks."

"Doesn't make me feel any less responsible. Destiny was one of my crew," he murmured. "I should have seen it coming… sensed something was off about her."

"Then let's make sure we do this right," I replied, nodding at the arriving police cars and emergency vehicles.

Abe stayed with us while we were attended to by the EMTs and gave law enforcement our account of the events. Two of the officers had already talked to Anna and Leah, so at least I wasn't starting from scratch. Honestly, I wasn't sure my head or my body could take much more. After being patched up—I was lucky to walk away with bruising and a nasty case of road rash—the EMTs agreed to release me into Abe's care, with the promise I would get properly checked out by a doctor once we reunited with the others.

But while I got a pass on a ride to the hospital, Blaze did not. After he was safely tucked into the ambulance, Abe helped me into the Ferrari. We did not stick around to watch the extraction of either bike or body, as Destiny deserved no more of our time and I had more pressing matters.

"I'll be glad when this is over," I said, closing my eyes as I leaned against the headrest.

"You don't think it is…over." It was not a question.

"Destiny may be dead but we don't have all the answers. In fact, it raises more questions. I don't think I can live with that— can you?" I opened one eye barely a slit and even that seemed a chore.

Abe shook his head as he glanced at me. "Something's nagging you. Lay it on me."

"Well, there are a few things, including Destiny's last words as she released my hand, 'you've nearly got this thing figured out. Now go get the rest.' It was a curious thing to say. Then again, she winked before the back of her head collided with a chunk of rock and her body was whipped about like a dog with a rope toy." I clucked my tongue, realizing how crass that sounded before adding, "Anyway, while she was obviously well versed in the art of deception, as well as being an extremely resourceful gal, I don't think she pulled this whole thing off by herself."

I paused to gauge Abe's reaction—hoping he wasn't going to change his mind about a trip to the hospital.

Mine.

"Why are you looking at me like that?" he asked, shaking his head when I covered my face with my t-shirt to hide my embarrassment, hoping I wasn't cracked. "Come on, AJ. Would you just get on with it, already? I don't think you're crazy, in case you were wondering. Not any crazier than usual, that is."

I smirked. "Okay, we can agree that Destiny was responsible for Decker's murder but at the time Cam was killed, there was no way she could have been at the beach. Blaze saw her at the bar. We could check with her bartender but I'm guessing that just prior to Bryce's accident—when his bike was tampered with—she was working. The same will probably be true for the other incidents. In fact, except for today—when she personally went to Bryce's to take Decker out—she was typically at the bar. She as much said so herself."

"So, who do you think this co-conspirator is—the mystery witness?" Abe asked.

"It's a definite possibility but..." I shrugged and Abe gestured for me to continue. "Another thing that's been bugging me and maybe I'm completely off base, but Destiny not only knew Decker long before Blaze hired her, she also knew that she was a private investigator. So how come no one else in the crew, including Cam, did?"

Abe swiveled his head, his eyes wide. "Come again?"

I told him about their interaction at the bar and the comment Destiny made to Decker in parting.

"You've got to be kidding."

"No, there's more. When we were talking about all the celebrities that have ventured into the bar, immortalized on the walls, Destiny made some off-hand comment about how it depends on how you define fame, nodding at a picture of a man that looked remarkably like Decker. He was clearly drunk and in a compromising situation with a pair of female…assets."

"Decker's father," Abe replied, blowing out a breath.

"At the time, I didn't think much of it but after everything, I started to wonder if there was a connection. Now, it looks like there is."

"And if Destiny knew about Decker all along…."

"Why didn't she tell Cam who Decker really was, especially considering all the threats and accidents that directly involved him? He most certainly would have mentioned Decker's arrival on the scene, that Blaze had hired someone outside the group on the crew, maybe even had an opinion about it."

Abe nodded. "True. You would think she would have said something, unless she had her own reasons for keeping Decker's identity under wraps."

"Exactly. And if Destiny wasn't candid with anyone about that, then everything else she said could be called into question," I replied.

"Like the laptop conveniently disappearing," Abe murmured.

I nodded. "It could have identified her partner-in-crime or pointed out any other discrepancies in her account of events that night. Destiny could have slipped something into his beverage and her partner could have collected him in the parking lot, driven him out to the beach, taken Cam out and then deposited both Blaze and his car in the appropriate locations before hitching a ride back."

Abe sat for a moment before responding "The thing I don't get, AJ, is why? You don't think Destiny was still pining over Blaze and wanted revenge, do you?"

I shrugged. "I think there was a plan already in motion and the film put a kink in the works. The fact that it turned out to be Blaze's film, was pure coincidence."

Abe narrowed his eyes as I told him about the model of the beach community we'd seen at the developers.

"And you think one of the bars in the model resembled Diamond Destiny's?" He asked when I finished.

I nodded. "A new, improved version of Diamond Destiny's, complete with custom surfboards on the front door. And if she'd been banking on the new digs and the project went away…"

"She may have felt she needed to resort…to murder," Abe finished, staring out the windshield.

I noticed we were getting close to Bryce's neighborhood and while I wanted to reunite with my friends, I did not wish to revisit the place where I'd lost another.

After a moment of silence, Abe turned to me. "Do you think Decker figured it all out, before?"

I broke from his gaze as I reflected on the last moment I had seen her alive. "I think she had all the pieces to the puzzle, even if she hadn't gotten them to fit just right."

Abe nodded, refocusing on the road. "At least she had that before she died."

I didn't tell him that I disagreed.

If she was anything like me—and I guessed she was—Decker wouldn't have been satisfied merely having the pieces, not when she knew she was so close. She would haunt us from the grave, until the puzzle was complete.

CHAPTER TWENTY-SIX

Our reunion was bittersweet.

Decker had been taken away but the aftermath of Destiny's destruction remained, not just in the charred structure that had once been Bryce's family's home but in my friends, who were sheathed in soot and covered in a myriad of cuts and scratches, lucky to have escaped alive.

Physically.

Emotionally, both had tear stains marring the soot on their faces and were quietly sitting on the sidewalk, arms wrapped around their legs as they awaited our arrival. Once Abe helped me out of the car, I limped to them and gave them each a fierce hug. As I pulled away from Leah, I tugged at the shorn ends of her hair.

"Heard you were offered some hair tips."

Leah snorted. "I shared some advice of my own."

I nodded, chuckling through cracked lips. "I'm sure you did. You okay, other than that?"

"You mean, except for the fact I thought I was faced with mothering a crazed Alaskan Malamute on my own?" she replied.

"I lived." I could offer her nothing more than a pained shrug and a wince. "There was a period of time…I thought neither of you did." I looked back at the house.

"I guess we're square, then." She sounded sad and a bit angry. "Damn Destiny," she said after a long moment, her voice filled with venom. "I'm glad she's dead."

"We're all okay, Leah." I gripped her arm. "Or we will be…someday."

"Decker might beg to differ," she replied bitterly. "At least tell me that witch suffered."

I wasn't prepared to tell her that I didn't think she had nor did I believe she had gotten what she deserved. Or had she?

"Were the investigators able to glean anything from all of this?"

Anna shook her head and frowned. "The house went up like a tinderbox and while Destiny may have pressed the button, the setup was probably outside her wheelhouse."

"So, even though that nasty witch is dead, her cohort is still out there," my best friend added, pummeling her thighs in frustration.

"That's the same conclusion AJ just drew," Abe replied, causing three sets of heads to turn in my direction.

He chuckled at my exasperated, exhausted expression, as I released a long breath.

"If you don't mind, I'll share your conclusions with everyone."

I gave him a "go ahead" gesture with my hands before slumping on the sidewalk. Anna and Leah huddled against me in an attempt to keep me upright. The Stantons remained standing as Abe relayed our previous discussion.

When he finished, Leah was the first to pipe up. "Before anyone finds out about her demise, we need to confirm a few things with Destiny's staff. One of us is also going to need to pose as Destiny and follow-up with the developer on the status of the project."

Of course, my best friend nominated herself.

While she dialed the developer's office, Anna offered to call the bar and moved out of earshot of Leah, who was already mid-stride in her Destiny impression. Though she dodged the admins, I worried that once she reached the inner sanctum and spoke to someone who'd actually met Destiny, they'd realize she was a fraud.

But even Abe and Elijah looked impressed as she sold her bill of lies. She was, after all, a concerned investor wanting to ensure the development had not been permanently derailed because of the "environmental nuts," as she called them.

Given the length of their conversation, the man on the other end didn't disappoint and seemed quite pleased that he was able to share the good news with her. After thanking him profusely, she turned and smirked.

"The gig's back on track." As Abe and Elijah started asking her questions, Leah put up a hand. "Come on boys, you can't both have me at once."

I rolled my eyes, causing her to chuckle. "Alright, I'll keep the intrigue to a minimum. Mr. Developer was pleased to announce that recent events have made it certain the environmentalists will not have a foot to stand on much longer. The previous snag, therefore, has become a moot point. To that end, all parties are interested in a speedy and amicable resolution, which will allow development to proceed as planned, likely within the next year to eighteen months."

"Interesting…it proves Destiny had a heck of a motive," Abe replied. "In order to ensure her dreams come to fruition, she needed to shut Blaze's documentary down."

Anna nodded as she listened to the tail-end of the conversation after she hung up from her own. "Here's more petrol to throw on Destiny's fire—according to the bartender, the laptop's been there all along. In fact, he was surprised when I said I was calling to see if there had been any word about its recovery."

"Sweet! We can take a look at the footage and finally get a line on our mystery dude," Leah replied.

Anna shook her head, frowning. "Looks like someone turned the system off—even the head bartender was surprised—couldn't think of a reason that any his co-workers would have done that."

"Mmm…hmm," I grumbled. "I'm sure we can think of a few million reasons. So, out of curiosity, when was the system conveniently taken offline?"

"The day the whole thing went down with Blaze," Anna replied, crossing her arms. "And that's not all. The bartender said before Blaze arrived, Cam had been in there for a brief period, too, and that he and Destiny had exchanged some heated words before he took off."

"Did have any idea what they were arguing about?" Elijah asked.

"Unfortunately, he did not," Anna murmured, brushing invisible dust from her cell phone's screen.

A black and white picture of Blaze popped up. He was standing alone at the beach, focusing on something in the distance, unaware she had captured him. She noticed me peering at the image and chuckled.

"He doesn't know I took this. I totally forgot I had it. Only found it while I was fidgeting, waiting for the police to question us after the EMTs gave us the thumbs up."

A familiar nagging flared up. "Anna, did Blaze send you a copy of the text with the drawing of the witness?"

Her eyes widened. "He did." She quickly thumbed through her gallery and once she'd found it, we all huddled around and peered at it.

"What is it, AJ?" Leah asked, dancing back and forth from one foot to the other.

"Can you pull up two pictures at once?" I glanced at Anna, who nodded. "Okay, let's place that drawing alongside Blaze's photo."

Though everyone was staring at me with mixed levels of curiosity, Anna complied, turning it around once the images were juxtaposed.

"You guys notice anything?" I asked, my heart thudding again my chest.

All of them glanced from one image to the next, finally Leah responded. "I suppose I can see the similarities, except for the nose and the hair, of course. But then again, I'm sure we could find similarities to *that* guy." She nodded at one of the investigators working the scene at the house.

I nodded. "Fair enough. Anna, how tall did they say the witness was?"

"About six-two. Why?"

"How tall would you say Blaze is?"

Anna tilted her head. "The same...wait, what are you suggesting?"

"Bear with me." I tapped my temple. "So the two are similar in height?"

This time, she squinted at me and not in a friendly sort of way, as she retracted the phone.

"Yes, but I don't like where you are going with this. You aren't suggesting Blaze and Destiny were working together? That he murdered—"

I held up a hand, realizing my misstep in trying to proceed cautiously. "Not Blaze, Anna, but someone who looks strikingly like him...knows him...knows Destiny...and is the same height as he is."

Leah smiled and nodded, wiggling her finger at me as she

caught where I was headed. "So much like brothers…most people thought they were cut from the same cloth."

Anna's hand flew to her mouth. "Oh, my God. It can't be! You're not saying…I mean, we saw—"

I shook my head. "Did we? Or perhaps, we saw what they wanted us to see."

The phone slid from her hand, hitting the pavement with a thud hard enough to have cracked the screen but amazingly, it didn't. Unlike Anna's phone, however, a relationship had fractured.

"Why?" she whispered.

I hated to say it probably came down to the oldest reason in the book.

And I wasn't talking about love.

CHAPTER TWENTY-SEVEN

Somewhere in the Midwest...weeks later...

It was time to collect Destiny's co-conspirator. Only this time it would take a whole other type of cavalry to take him down.

We'd planned it for weeks.

Admittedly, we hadn't planned it—the FBI took on that component—but from the start, we insisted on being front and center when it went down.

We must have made a compelling argument—our request was grudgingly granted with the understanding that we would not, in fact, be allowed front and center but could witness the operation from a safe, FBI-approved distance.

We'd always known we'd be fighting an uphill battle, the first being that they'd find our story believable. After they took their own sweet time double-checking our facts, however, they created a task force that would take the story to its conclusion. It helped that local law enforcement and the M.E.'s office had corroborated our suspicions and that the developer had been not only forth-coming but surprisingly cooperative as the investigation unfolded.

Unfortunately, there was nothing more that could have been gleaned from Destiny. Prior to her untimely, though justly deserved death, she had been particularly careful in clipping any threads that could have unraveled her complicity any more than we already had, leaving investigators to work the knots out on their own—one knot, in particular.

Of course, the Feds had to locate him first. But as it turned out, what they say about hiding in plain sight was truer than we could have imagined and made for a riveting—and satisfying—ending.

So on a hazy day, not long after we'd come together to escort Blaze out of the hospital we stood, seven abreast along the crest of the hill, looking down at the residence at a safe, FBI-approved distance, just as we'd been instructed.

A wave of emotions buzzed throughout our little group.

Though he'd been surprisingly calm when we'd initially shared our theory, Blaze now impatiently resituated his crutches.

Anna, who held his hand on one side and mine on the other, remained stoic.

Holding Leah's hand on the other side in addition to Nicoh's lead, I spent my time shifting from foot to foot.

Leah tugged at the ends of her hair with her free hand while chewing an entire pack of gum harder than it deserved.

Abe and Elijah whispered excitedly, giving a play-by-play of the action unfolding below as they peered through binoculars.

We watched as a woman and her three children left in a luxury SUV. All of them had been bundled up and laughing and I wondered what adventure awaited them. Whatever it was, when they returned home, their lives would never be the same.

"Do you think she had any idea?" I asked of no one in particular.

It was Abe who replied, having been the primary in dealing with the FBI. "They said it would be hard to prove but they think so." He glanced at Blaze who continued to stare at the family as they pulled down the drive, before continuing, "We have confirmation from her parents—who own this McMansion—that when he told her to take the kids and leave town, she would be doing so for good and that she could never make contact with anyone from their lives in L.A. ever again."

"Destiny must have paid him well," Leah murmured.

"It was a means to an end," Anna replied, her frown as sour as her tone. "She wanted to get out of that dump and into a shiny new bar and considering he was in a world of hurt financially and needed the money, he made the perfect partner."

Just then, a man dressed in running attire exited the house, waving what looked like a collection of lunch bags until the woman pulled the SUV to a stop and rolled down the window as he approached. He handed her the bags, then leaned in to kiss her, laughing. She reached out and grabbed him by the face, kissing him again before rolling the window up. He smiled and waved to them as they exited the driveway and pulled onto the adjoining road. Once they had disappeared, he ran back toward the house and used the porch as a frame for stretching, seemingly without a care in the world.

"Feds confirmed the parents are on an extended vacation, an Alaskan cruise," Abe commented, though no one had asked.

The man finished his stretches and had just plugged his earbuds in when the task force emerged from behind the hedges, trees and outbuildings that surrounded the property.

If he was surprised, he made no show, raising his hands and lying flat on his belly calmly as instructed. Soon, he was hand-cuffed and it was over as quickly as it had started.

Though the story had drawn to a close, I felt little sense of resolution. There had been no happy ending.

The silence of the group mirrored my own sentiment.

Finally, Abe spoke, "Steep price to pay. For all of them."

"Maybe they figured they had no choice," Blaze replied, though his voice was void of conviction.

I surprised myself when I added, "There's always a choice."

Blaze nodded and released a small chuckle. "You're starting to sound like Decker."

I snorted. "I'd kind of like to think she would've approved."

As though sensing our presence, Bryce squinted up at the ridge before the agent tucked him in the back of the cruiser and continued to stare as they pulled away and traveled up the drive.

Suddenly, the sky broke open and rain poured down, blanketing us with its cool, refreshing wetness.

Apparently, at the end of the day Decker did, indeed, approve.

Two days later…back in L.A.

I finally got my California sunset but it didn't turn out quite the way I had envisioned.

After Blaze and Anna reconciled, agreeing that the beach where Cam's ashes had been shared with the ocean he loved so much would far exceed any other location for their lifelong commitment to one another, I found myself there on one afternoon, for an entirely different type of commitment.

As I was packing for our return trip to Phoenix, anticipating a long overdue reconciliation with my bed, I received an unexpected phone call from Officer Piedmont, Decker's childhood friend. Prior to her untimely death, she had mentioned our discussion of a meet and greet between Mia and Nicoh once the case had been resolved. Now that he was the guardian of his best friend's canine companion, he wanted to honor her wishes.

Though he'd caught me off-guard with his proposition, I quickly agreed, knowing that it would not only do a world of good for Mia but for Peedy, too, as they had both lost the most important human in their lives.

I hadn't seen him at the crash site and truth be told even if I had, I probably wouldn't haven't remembered, given all the chaos of that night.

So I was pleasantly surprised as he approached, boyishly cute in his t-shirt, board shorts and flip flops—a tall, tanned drink of California, with sun-kissed curls barely tamed by the crop of his haircut and which only enhanced the aquamarine brilliance of the eyes staring back at me. A flash of white emerged as he broke into a massive grin, revealing dimples and a small scar that passed from his lower lip to the base of the cleft of his chin.

"From the description Decker gave me"—he immediately blushed, composing himself as he looked down—"of this big guy, you must be Arianna."

"Please, call me AJ," I replied, extending my hand, "and this is Nicoh."

He nodded and clasped my hands with his own, which were warm but firm. "Nice to meet you, AJ. Logan. And Mia."

The statuesque German Shepherd flipped her tail and cocked her head, giving her canine counterpart a thorough once over. Nicoh murmured low whoo-whoo, which I translated to "ooooh, she's pretty," before huffing out a breath as he swooshed his tail from side to side while dancing from one paw to the next.

"Mind your manners, Buddy," I replied. "Mia will put you in your place if you don't behave."

Nicoh released another huff before bowing his head and leaning in so that Mia could sniff. She did, and after a wagging of tails, they took account of one another in typical canine fashion.

Of course, both of the humans blushed and I managed to awkwardly squawk out, "Don't worry, I don't think they'll be offended if we don't follow suit."

I winced at my choice of words but Logan chuckled easily, adding, "Yeah, I think a handshake should suffice. For now, at least." His eyes widened. "Err…what I meant was—"

I waved him off and we laughed, now that each of us had put our foot into it, we had effectively broken the ice, if not melted it.

We walked up the beach, the dogs side by side as Logan told me a bit about growing up in the valley, reminiscing about adventures with his best friend. It was easy to see how much they had cared about one another, fought for one another, loved one another.

"I'm curious, how exactly did you get the nickname Peedy, anyway?" I asked, though I'd assumed it was short for Piedmont, betting that he caught crap for it each time Decker used it in front of his peers.

Logan tossed his head back and laughed. Hard. Pretty soon he had me laughing again, too.

"What?" I finally managed to snort out.

"It's not 'Peedy.' It's P.D., as in the initials P and D?" He paused to chuckle again, after taking in my confused expression. "It stands for Piedmont and Decker. I called her the same thing. We always pretended we'd grow up to be detectives like our pops and form our own agency. Like Simon and Simon but without the whole sibling rivalry thing."

"I would imagine," I replied. "Close enough to the truth, though." Logan nodded. "You ever consider it? Leaving law enforcement, opening your own agency?"

Logan looked out at the ocean. "To be honest, I just don't think it would be the same without her…without D."

"I know it feels that way now, Logan. But, maybe you should keep your options—and that door—open. I think Decker would want you to."

"Maybe, someday." He shrugged before turning to me. "Why, are you offering to be my partner?"

I laughed. "I think I already have my hands full—between my photography business, my saucy best friend and…this guy." I waved a hand at Nicoh, who was acting about as goofy as I felt as he trotted to keep up with the beauty at his side.

"Well, it would be immensely useful, considering you clearly already have a considerable skill set under your belt," Logan teased.

I snorted. "It takes a considerable amount of patience, persistence and downright stubbornness—honed over years of dedication to mastering the craft."

He released a chuckle and nodded. "I would guess so."

We walked in a comfortable silence for a few moments, until I shared what had been weighing on me. "Seriously, Logan, at least take what I've said into consideration about hanging up a shingle. I think it suits you. And I think Decker would agree."

"You do the same, AJ, if you change your mind about hanging that shingle with me?" I smiled and nodded, becoming self-conscious when I noticed he was studying me. "Now I know why Decker chose you."

"Chose me?" I stopped, nearly tripping over my own feet in the process.

Logan grabbed my elbow to ensure I remained upright. "You remind me so much of her." He chuckled. "Except for the two left feet, that is."

"Thanks," I replied, brushing hair out of my eyes. "It's one of my handier skills—tripping over my own feet, that is. You'll never know when you'll need that one in pinch." Logan laughed, causing me to blush. Again. "Anyway you are right, I'm sure Decker typically had both feet firmly planted and always knew which direction she was traveling before she took the next step."

He nodded. "She was also an exceptional judge of character. The day before she was…killed, she wanted to make sure I passed along a message—a request—in the event something happened to her."

"An ominous bit of foreshadowing," I murmured, prodding Logan to continue. "This request…"

"She wants you to look into her mother's case," he replied, searching my eyes, his tone serious.

"Her mother's—what?" I stammered. "Why me?"

"Decker said the two of you shared something in common. Something…deeply personal."

"Death," I whispered, thinking of my parents, my sister, my friends.

"It not just death that connects you, AJ," he replied, holding my shoulders so that I was forced to face him. "It's the way they died."

"They were murdered," I replied. Logan nodded. "Where… how would I know where to start?" Panic washed over me, not wishing to let Decker or her faith in me down.

"With both feet firmly planted, confident that you know what direction you're taking before you take that step."

I looked down, frowning when I realized he was using my own words against me.

He tilted my chin until I met his eyes.

"And with your assistance?" I asked, disappointed when he shook his head. "Because you can't? Or won't?"

"Because I'm a cop," he replied, his tone sad but earnest. "I can, however, offer you a starting point."

"A lead?" My reply came out sounding far more hopeful than I felt. Before he could respond, I spouted out, "Why not take it to the Stanton's—or Anna? This is more their level of expertise."

"No, AJ, she wanted you." Logan released a breath before continuing, "Besides, there's a serious conflict of interest where they're concerned. As it is, there will be hell to pay when this comes out."

"I'm not sure I like the sound of that. Maybe you should just tell me about this lead Decker had."

"It's more than just a lead, AJ. Decker had a name."

"Okay…" I gestured for him to continue, even though I was still not convinced I wanted to know, regardless of how far this name, whoever's it was, took me.

"Terrence Edwards," he replied, ensuring he had my full attention before he added, "The man who changed Decker and her pop's lives forever.

"Until this moment, that bastard has gotten away with murder."

~ The End ~

ABOUT HARLEY

Harley Christensen lives in Phoenix, Arizona with her significant other and their mischievous motley crew of rescue dogs (aka the "kids").

When not at her laptop, Christensen is an avid hockey fan and lover of all things margarita. It's also rumored she's never met a green chile or jalapeño she didn't like, regardless of whether it liked her back.

For more information on the author and her books, please visit her at www.mischievousmalamute.com.